LOVE ME
IN THE DARK

MIA ASHER

Love Me In the Dark

Published by Mia Asher

Copyright © 2017 by Mia Asher

Photographer: Wong Sim

Model: Amadeo Leandro

Cover Design by Hang Le of Designs by Hang Le

Formatting by Kassi Snider of Kassi Jean Formatting and Design

For L and J and K.
This book ~~book~~ wouldn't be here without you.

PART ONE

PROLOGUE
SÉBASTIEN

Ten years ago ...

I'M STRUMMING MY FINGERS on the windowsill, watching the rain fall outside the apartment, when I feel small, warm arms hugging me from behind.

"Good morning," she says hoarsely before placing a kiss on my shoulder.

I cover her hands with mine, enjoying the feel of her naked body pressed against me. "Sleep well?"

"Like a rock."

"I didn't know rocks snored."

She bites my shoulder. "Idiot," she adds teasingly.

Chuckling, I reach for her and bring her to stand in front of me. "Hello," I say, kissing the tip of her nose. A halo of fire frames her delicate features accentuating the milky whiteness of her skin and the blue of her eyes. Poppy Smith.

I met her over two years ago when she spilled hot coffee on my lap by "accident." According to her, I was rude to one of her coworkers at the coffee shop where she worked, so she wanted to put me in my place. It's funny because at first, I didn't even notice her, but as my gaze rested on her slim, coltish figure covered in colorful clothes that didn't match, her chipped manicure, and her peaceful yet stubborn features, I was a goner. I never stood a chance against Poppy and her thirst for life.

"Hello." She pushes herself away from me and makes her way back to bed. I'm watching her perfect ass, imagining what I've done to it, when she glances back and smiles a smile full of promises, the kind to drive one to an early grave. I don't know what I did to get so damn lucky, but thank you, Jesus. You're the man.

"Hungry?"

My breathing accelerates as my cock stirs awake, blood pumping hard. Need and want palpable in the air. "Starving."

She lies down on the bed, spreading her legs apart. Her fingers begin to trace a small path down to my fucking heaven. An enticing grin on her beautiful face, she gives me a saucy look. "Why are you still standing there, then? Come over here and have your breakfast."

Again, thank you, Jesus. I owe you a big one. I join her in no time, moving to lie down next to her. I take her in my arms, kissing the curve where her neck and shoulder meet, a place that I've claimed as mine.

I remember the news from last night. "Wait ..." I splay my fingers across her growing stomach, feeling primal pride and happiness. "Hello there, buddy. Can you hear us? It's your very horny dad," I whisper against Poppy's skin while showering kisses on her jawline. "Time to put those earmuffs on, little one."

Poppy laughs softly as she places a hand behind my neck, pulling me toward her, rubbing herself on my cock—lighting me up like Fourth of July fireworks. "How about Daddy does less talking and more ..."

The rest of her words get lost between my lips when I cover her body with mine, silencing her with my mouth, with my tongue, with my never-ending need. A lifetime spent like this, in our bed, our limbs tangled like a rope, sweat on our skin, and full of each other would never be enough for me. Even if I lived a thousand lifetimes, it still wouldn't be enough.

After we spend the rest of the morning satiating our bodies, we begrudgingly get out of bed. Poppy goes to take a shower while my gaze lingers on the twisted, guilty sheets. I'm tempted to call Poppy's parents and make up an excuse as to why we can't make it after all, then join my girlfriend in the shower. However, I stop myself. Poppy misses them, and she should go home for a visit. Shaking my head, I sigh, get dressed, and go downstairs. Once I finish packing her car in the rain, we stand in the kitchen ready to say goodbye. I'm going to join her tomorrow after I drop off a few paintings at a gallery, and together we'll share the news with them.

"Drive safely," I say, staring out of the window. The wind has picked up, and the rain is falling harder than earlier in the day.

"It's a short drive to Kent." She wraps her arms around my waist and leans her head on my chest. "I can make it with my eyes closed. Don't worry about it, sir."

I pull her closer to me, suddenly afraid to let her go. "*Il n'y a qu'un bonheur dans la vie, c'est d'aimer et d'être aimé.*"

There is only one happiness in life, to love and be loved.

"Are you trying to get lucky again?" Poppy rubs her cheek on my shirt, a small smile playing on her face. "Because let me tell you, quoting George Sand will definitely get you laid."

"Maybe." I lower my head and bury my nose in her hair. I take a deep breath, filling my lungs with her essence. "Is it working?"

"You have no idea." She kisses my chest. "Unfortunately, Mum made me promise her that I'd be there for tea, and if I don't leave now, I'll never make it. Peter's bringing his new girlfriend."

"What happened to Millie?"

"Who knows. But I'll make it up to you tomorrow?" she asks, lowering her hand and running her fingers along the front of my jeans. Slowly. Decadently.

"Good God, woman. You're going to be the death of me," I groan, closing my eyes momentarily.

Giggling, she stands on her tiptoes and cups my cheeks with her hands. "*Je t'aime*, my horny man," she says before pressing her lips against mine, kissing me with everything that she is.

My woman.

My life.

After I say goodbye to Poppy and watch her drive away, I head to the bedroom. As I'm going up the stairs, there's a sharp pang in the middle of my chest. *Must be the Indian food we had last night,* I think as I rub the pain away in circles. When it's passed, I finish climbing the few remaining steps that lead to the room. I walk to the closet, pull out an old battered shoebox, and open it, finding what I'm looking for. Heart drumming in my chest, I take out the small velvet box that holds my happiness and put it in the front pocket of my jeans.

Tomorrow.

A few hours later …

I see Peter's incoming call.

"Bonjour, fucker," I say over the phone, looking at the diamond ring in my hand, smiling as I picture Poppy's surprise when she sees it. Some people might say we're too young to get married or to start a family, but what the hell do they know? When you meet the one person who gives your life meaning, who makes you a better man so you can be worthy of her love, you don't wait for the "right time" to come along. You jump. You run. You fly.

"Has Pops arrived yet? She's not answering her phone—"

"Sébastien … you need to come home …" Peter's voice sends a chill running down my spine. "We're at the hospital. It's Poppy …"

And just like that, my world goes dark.

CHAPTER
ONE

Do you ever look at yourself in the mirror and not recognize your reflection?

A flawless woman stares back at me. She has long caramel brown hair blown out to perfection, and her formerly curvaceous body is now trim and slim and outfitted in a designer dress. She's someone worthy of William Alexander Fitzpatrick IV.

My husband.

Gone are the traces of the wild girl I once was. The one who felt too much, laughed too loud, ate too much, while juggling work and college. Her hips were a little too large, her mouth a little too wide, and her curly hair had a life of its own. She was broke, lived in a shoebox, yet couldn't have been happier. Peanut butter and jelly sandwiches and cheap box wine kept her fed and sane.

I chuckle sadly. I didn't have much other than my dreams, but it was enough for me. Because in those dreams, I would finish college with a kick-ass job that would pay me enough money to get my own apartment, nice shoes, and great wine. I would also become the next Mrs. Brad Pitt.

My arms outstretched, I'd danced to the vibrant music of life.

I prayed for romance, adventure, the unknown. I wanted to fall in love and love to the point of no return. I wanted the turmoil, the stress, the upheaval, and chaos—the Sturm und Drang. And my God wasn't deaf. He, with his almighty ways, granted me all my wishes. While crying over lattes with my best friend, Sailor, about my latest break-up, I met *him*. Halfway through my sob story, I heard him chuckle behind his newspaper.

"Excuse me," I said affronted. "What's so funny?"

The man lowered the newspaper and placed it on the table next to him. At the sight of his handsome face, I felt my cheeks grow hot while forgetting why I was so offended. He stood and made his way from the couch area to our table. Older than me, the man walked like a king, an emperor. Larger than life, he seemed to know his worth. With his expensive suit, tall form, perfectly wavy combed blond hair, and even more perfect features, the man radiated power and wealth. I couldn't have looked away even if I'd wanted to.

He gave me his card while his bright blue eyes took in my tear-stained face. "If you call me, I promise not to make you cry." He smiled dazzlingly, turned on his feet, and walked out of the store, leaving Sailor and me with our mouths half open.

I lasted a week before I gave in and called him.

It was a whirlwind romance fit for the movies. The kind you dreamed of when you were a little girl playing with dolls. It was surreal, breathtaking, and it was happening to me. We had a lavish wedding on my twenty-second birthday with celebrations that lasted for days.

I never got that dream job I wanted so much. Instead, I tried to become the perfect wife. I tossed my old clothes and went shopping at Bergdorf's for new items worthy of my life with William. And if sometimes I mourned my past life, I reminded myself that there was no room for the old Valentina in this one.

"Valentina?"

Lost in thought, I hear William saying my name. I give my head a tiny shake and turn towards his voice. All it takes is one look from my husband, handsome in dress slacks and a white button-down shirt, to bring back hundreds of memories, good, bad, and ugly. And the love I felt—the love I still feel—for him comes rushing back like a tsunami. And like a tsunami, its strong current continues to pull me down repeatedly.

How I fell for him. William Alexander Fitzpatrick IV. He was polished and with a pedigree that could rival the Kennedy's.

Princeton grad. Walking Ralph Lauren ad. Hedge fund whiz. Trust-fund baby.

He was everything that I wasn't, and he wanted me. He *chose* me. Me.

Valentina. On a scholarship at my dream university in New York City. Savvy concession and thrift store shopper. I was comfortable in my own skin and knew my own worth. Yet I couldn't help but be surprised that William wanted me, and that he returned my love unconditionally. In a world built on dreams, he became my one truth.

"Hi." I turn to face the mirror, looking at my reflection. Dispassionately, I notice my hands shaking as I try to put a diamond stud on my left earlobe. "I thought you'd already left?"

"Did you forget what today is?" he asks softly.

"Monday?" I look at the Rolex on my wrist, noting the time. "I'm running late for breakfast with the girls. They must be at the club already."

"Valentina …" William steps behind me, his front touching my back, and runs his hands over my arms, leaving goose bumps in their wake. "It's our anniversary, my love."

My lower lip quivers as I look up to see my husband in all his golden, virile beauty. In the mirror, his blue eyes meet mine, and there's sadness and sorrow in them. And guilt. So much fucking guilt. I'm surprised we're both not drowning in it.

But it wasn't always the case.

At the beginning of our life together as a married couple, we fought hard, fucked harder, loved hardest. And when our eyes met, I saw life, tenderness, and a bright future ahead of us.

Little did I know, little did I understand, that in the balance of life, happiness can't exist without sadness.

"Oh. We can celebrate tonight. I promised the girls—"

"Stay," he says hoarsely as he spins me around to face him.

He gets down on his knees between my legs and showers my stomach with slow kisses that burn me from the inside out. I would love nothing more than to run my fingers through his hair, feeling its softness, its warmth, but I can't bring myself to touch him. Not today. His large hands cup my ass from behind, pushing me closer to his mouth. He breathes me in. Swallows me whole. His lips taste through the fabric of my skirt the flavor that belongs to him. My body screams *I am his, I am his.*

But my heart hasn't forgotten.

One day, right before our tenth anniversary, I decided to surprise my husband with an impromptu lunch at our townhouse in the city.

I got take-out from our favorite sushi place, flowers from the deli next door, and sped to our place on Park Avenue. My plan was to give him a call and ask him to meet me there. Maybe, after lunch, we could spend the rest of the afternoon naked in bed.

I laughed at myself as anticipation and excitement ran freely in my veins. I couldn't remember when was the last time I did something so spontaneous. It didn't matter. It felt great.

I was married to the love of my life.

We were in love.

Life couldn't get any better.

Turns out it was me who walked into a surprise. There, in the middle of our newly renovated kitchen stood my husband, hands on his intern's head as she took him in her mouth.

I wish I could say that I divorced his sorry ass, but that would be a lie.

I loved him too much—too blindly—to walk away.

I had given him twelve years of my life. Our marriage was everything I had—it was an extension of me. My identity. His breathing was my breathing. His dreams were my dreams. His happiness was my happiness.

Who was Valentina without William? I no longer remember, and the thought of finding out terrified me. So I made lemonade out of lemons. I forgave him and tried to pretend it never happened.

But it had, and I couldn't forget—I still can't. It's been a year since the day I realized that not all love stories have a happy ending.

My aunt used to tell me that trust was like a plate. Once it was broken, it didn't matter how much glue you used to put it back together; it would never be the same. So here I am holding onto the broken fragments of our love—our marriage—trying not to cut myself with them.

Some days are better than others. Sometimes I'm full of hate and resentment and can't look at his face without feeling disgust and betrayal. And sometimes when he touches me like he used to, I can fool myself into thinking I imagined the whole thing. But even after all this time, when William places his hands on my head like he did to her that day, I relive it all over again.

Enough.

I give my head a tiny shake while feeling William unzip my skirt, letting it fall to the floor, and tugging my thong to the side. The room swirls around me. My legs grow weak, and I press my back to the mirror for support. I want to tell him to stop, that I don't want him touching me, but I can't bring myself to do it. Tongue-tied, I get lost in the unforgiving, sensual disarming of my body at his hands. My will dissolves. He's on his knees while I remain standing, but it's me who crumbles on the inside with each minute that passes.

Love is cruel for it makes one weak.

And William continues to punish me for it over and over again.

Moments pass and everything ceases to exist except for the both of us. William pulls me down onto the soft carpeted floor. His hands on me. His tongue moving inside me along with his punishing fingers. I bite my lip hard to stop a moan from escaping until I can taste blood. But it's him I feel outside and inside this body of mine—he's everywhere.

Obliterating light consumes me, and I come undone with his name on my tongue. He kneels over me and fists his cock, pumping it up and down fast and hard until his warm seed spills on my skin and a groan is torn from his chest.

We're now lying on the carpeted floor, exhausted and bathed in the remnants of our lovemaking.

His fingers stroke my shoulder. "I have something for you."

"Oh?"

He gets up, goes to his nightstand, and takes something out of its drawer. Package in hand, he comes back. "Here," he says, handing me a white envelope.

Part of me wishes I could tell William that he doesn't need to shower me with gifts. I don't need anything. All I want—all I've ever wanted—is his love. I sit up and cross my legs. "I didn't get you anything."

"It's all right." He buries his hands inside the front pockets of his unzipped trousers that hang loosely around his hips. "Go on, open it."

I follow his orders and find a key inside. I take it out and inspect it, turning it this way and that. "What's this?"

"A key," he adds with dry amusement.

"I can see that, but what's it for?"

"It's the key to an apartment in Paris."

"We're going to Paris?"

He nods, caressing my cheek with the back of his hand. "I have to go for work next week. And I'd like you to come with me."

"You do?" I hate the fact that my voice is heavy with surprise and wonder, but I can't remember the last time my husband sought my company during one of his trips.

"Yes, darling. Once my meetings are over, I can take a few weeks off, and we can spend the rest of the time having fun. What do you say, Val? Just you and me. No distractions. Away from everything. Like it used to be."

"Like it used to be …" I let the words roll around my tongue, rediscovering their taste. "Do you think that's even possible?"

"I don't know, but we can try." He sits down on the floor next to me and pulls me on top of him, his arms going around me. The all-encompassing hug robs me of the air I need to breathe. Burying his nose in my hair, he lets out a suppressed sigh. "I want things to go back to how they were before I …" He clears his throat. "Before I fucked up."

"Do you really mean that?" I ask, afraid to open the doors of my heart again and let him back in.

"Darling, listen to me. It's been a couple of shitty years, but I love you. No more pretending that things are fine this time. Let's actually work through our problems."

"I want to believe you, but … but I'm afraid, William."

"I understand. How about this? Let's start in Paris. And when we come back, hell, I'll even go to couple's therapy with you." His palm cups my flat, empty stomach. "It might also be time to start filling our nursery."

"Oh, William." My voice breaks. "You really mean that?"

"Yes, darling."

I cup his cheeks with shaky hands, the seeds of hope taking root in my soul. "Like it used to be, huh?"

"No." He smiles his charming and dazzling smile that I fell in love with. "It will be even better." He lowers his face and kisses me. It's long and tender. Sweet and slow. It's a kiss full of forgiveness and the promise of new beginnings.

Lost in his embrace, the ice surrounding my heart thaws completely, and I let him back in.

CHAPTER TWO

"Madame, we're here," the driver says with a heavily French-accented English.

Snapping out of my reverie, I realize that we're parked outside a very elegant building. There's a plaque on the black gate surrounding it that says Avenue Foch. I feel butterflies in my stomach. This is where we will begin rebuilding our marriage from the ashes.

While I watch Pierre get out of the car and make his way to my door, my phone begins to vibrate. I take it out of my Birkin and see that it's a text message from William.

William: Are you at the apartment yet?

Me: Just about. I'm outside the building. It's beautiful.

William: I'm glad you like it. I miss you.

I smile. Such simple words, but they fill me with happiness. To know that he misses me—that he cares.

Me: I miss you, too. Can't wait for you to be here.

William: I'll be there tomorrow.

Me: I'll be the naked woman on the bed. Waiting for you.

William: God, Val. You're killing me.

I grin, slightly blushing. Me: Good. Hurry up.

William: I'm not going to let you out of bed for days, you know?

Me: I'm holding you to it.

Pleasure and desire swirl around me like an intoxicating perfume as Pierre opens the door and I get out of the black Mercedes. I pause for a moment to look around. There's a pretty park across the street and more residential buildings in the surrounding area. Emotions heightened, the beauty and the romance of the Parisian architecture become even more breathtaking.

"Could you please take my suitcases to the apartment?" I say, handing him the key. "I'd like to stay out here a little longer."

"*Oui*, madame."

I watch him go inside the building before focusing on the empty park across the street once more. There's a light, cool breeze rustling the leaves of the trees, making them dance. Mesmerized, their music envelops me. I pretend they are whispering their secrets to me, telling me that I've come to the right place, that we're doing the right thing. And slowly, very slowly, hope spreads its warm light like a new dawn. I take a deep breath enjoying the view a little longer, then follow Pierre inside, a new spring in my step.

Pierre has placed my suitcases in the bedroom and is waiting for my next orders. I browse the place William has rented indefinitely, admiring the elegant décor. The furniture and walls are shades of ice white and cool grays. Everything matches. Everything is pleasing to the eye.

I trace a gleaming wood table sitting in the middle of the foyer with the back of my fingers. "Wow. This place is something else."

Pierre nods in agreement. "Would that be all, madame?"

I remove my trench coat. "Yes, thank you so much."

When he's in front of me, he extends a hand with a card in it. "Here's my number. Call whenever you need me. Your husband's assistant hired me for the entirety of your stay in Paris."

"You'll definitely be hearing from me." I take it from him and run my fingers on the cool paper, chuckling lightly. "I don't even know where to go food shopping."

We go over tomorrow's schedule, and as he's getting ready to leave, I notice the time. Noting it's still relatively early, I realize that I don't want to stay in. I'm in Paris after all. Paris! Excitement courses through me, making my body hum.

"One second, Pierre."

With one hand on the door handle, Pierre glances in my direction. "Yes?"

"I think I'd like to go out for dinner."

He lets go of the handle and turns to face me. "Would you like me to wait for you until you're ready to go out?"

"Oh, no, no need for that. I'd like to do some exploring on my own, actually. I was just wondering if you could recommend a place nearby with live music and great food? I don't want to get lost on my first day here."

"Of course. There's a nice place not far from here. Great food. Sometimes they have a live band on the weekends."

"Sounds perfect."

"It's straight down the road. You can't miss it."

After Pierre writes down the name and the directions to the restaurant, he takes his leave, I jump in the shower, thoughts of a delicious dinner already filling my head. Once my hair and makeup are taken care of, I choose a form-fitting short white dress with a cape and nude heels.

Clutch in hand, I leave the apartment behind and set out into the night. I'm a ball of nerves and crazy exhilaration and, maybe, a little fear.

I reach the restaurant without a problem. The place is low-key yet stylish, bathed in an amber haze, the aroma of truffle oil and butter float in the air. The people, lost in their own conversations fueled by wine and a good time, are dressed elegantly. To my left, near the floor to ceiling windows, there's a band playing a jazzy tune. I smile. *This is exactly what I was looking for.*

I spot a svelte young brunette behind the hostess stand talking to a couple. As I wait for my turn, I hear that she's speaking in English. Thank goodness. When the man and woman step to the side, I move to the counter.

"Hello, I was wondering if there's a table available for one."

"Bonjour," she answers politely, looking at the computer screen in front of her. "There's about an hour's wait for the next open table."

I thank her after she writes my name down, and head to the bar, which seems to be as crowded as the rest of the restaurant. There isn't one seat available, and there's a large group of people surrounding it like a barricade. Sighing, I remember seeing an open gallery next door. A more pleasurable idea forms in my head. Maybe I can take a quick look in there to pass the time instead.

As soon as I step in, I immediately realize the big mistake I've made. It appears like I just crashed a party, maybe the opening of an art exhibit. Everywhere I look there are people dressed to the nines. Waiters balancing trays full of drinks and hors d'oeuvres, and a violinist wanders the room playing what I believe is Mozart. It's beautiful.

I'm about to leave when my eyes land on a painting to my left that makes me stop in my tracks. Hypnotized, every part of my me demands to see it up close. I hesitate, remembering that I don't have an invitation, but dismiss the thought as quickly as it comes. I shouldn't offend anyone as long as I'm quick and I don't have anything to eat or drink.

The noise fades when I'm standing in front of it. It's a lone poppy flower crushed on the ground, droplets of rain falling around it. The colors are dark, intense, the brush strokes powerful, angry. It makes me think of life and how fragile it is. One day you're young and beautiful and the next you're dying alone, forgotten, on the cold, hard ground.

I'm still absorbed in the painting when I feel someone's presence behind me.

"Excusez-moi," a woman addresses me in not such a friendly tone.

Shit.

Dread lodges in my stomach as I turn slowly, so very slowly, to face the slim woman dressed in black now standing in front of me. And yep, I was right. She looks pissed off.

An apology on my tongue, the woman starts to spew accusations in fast, heated French. She's getting louder and louder. Out of the corner of my eyes, I notice that we're drawing a lot of attention. Even the violinist has stopped playing. This would be a perfect time for the ground to open up and swallow me whole.

"I'm sorry," I mutter nervously, raising my hands in peace. I close my eyes momentarily, cursing my clumsiness for not knowing French. "I'm so sorry," I repeat, embarrassed and uncomfortable. "I don't understand what you're saying, but I'm going to leave now. I'm *really, really* sorry."

She draws the attention of some very serious, angry looking men, maybe the security personnel, points irately toward me and the door. As they begin to stride toward us, I back off, fear making my steps unsure. "I'm going to leave now. No need to escort me out." *God, I need to get out of here.*

Blindly, I turn on my feet when an arm snakes around my waist, taking me by surprise. Before I know what's happening, I find myself pressed against a firm body. Shock courses through me as I raise my gaze to look at the man. The most vivid blue eyes I've ever seen focus on me, making me feel oddly unbalanced and short of breath. I stand there unmoving, figuratively and literally caught. His arms are like corded steel wrapping around my waist and pulling me closer to him. I gasp at the sensation of his hard body against the softness of mine. And as our gazes lock, a hot blush paints my cheeks bright red.

"There you are, beautiful," the man says in perfect English, the slight trace of a French accent lurking in his voice. He smiles, an easy smile full of mischief, and I feel like I'm falling and falling. "I've been looking for you."

Huh?

He lowers his head close to my ear and whispers, "Just go with the flow."

"Wha—"

He takes my mouth in a kiss I feel all the way to my bones. My eyes widen in surprise. I try to push him away, but he lets go of my waist and tangles his hands in my hair, his fingers cradling my head, and brings us closer as though he was trying to fuse us into one. He slants his lips over mine, so the kiss becomes deeper, needier. His tongue pushes past my resistance, ready to conquer and take and take. And as it tangles with mine unashamedly and unapologetically, I can't move. I can't think. Shock and anger slowly melt into surrender. I'm rendered useless by the man ravishing my mouth and senses. Somewhere in my mind, there's a small yet wise voice telling me to put a stop to it because this is wrong, to end the kiss before it consumes me.

But I ignore it all.

Because as his lips continue to savage mine, an inexplicable yearning so intense it shocks me comes over my being. I find myself kissing him back, needing more until he pulls away as though I was burning him.

"Well, I'll be damned," he says. His bright eyes roam my face, my lips, my cheeks, my eyes. He raises a trembling hand to run through his hair. Then, as though he's remembered where we are, he grins slowly, throws his arm over my shoulders, and turns to face the lady who was yelling at me before. Dazed and confused, I blink a couple of times while trying to get my bearings. What just happened?

"Margot," he addresses her. He winks at me before letting go of my waist. I see a window of opportunity to get away. I'm about to move when he places a hand possessively on the curve of my hip, obstructing my retreat.

"Don't even think about it," he whispers in my ear before he leans down, running his nose and lips along the side of my ear down to my shoulder. His touch raises goose bumps all over my skin, making my insides feel all tingly.

"I see you've met my date," he says to Margot, his voice sure and smooth.

She crosses her arms over her chest, the golden bracelets adorning her thin wrists digging into her skin, and replies something in French.

Breathless and shaken to the core, I watch my French chevalier while making the very unpleasant discovery that he is, in fact, extremely attractive, although he looks more like the wicked villain in a novel with his swarthy looks than the knight in shining armor. A man's face shouldn't be that sinful, his body that virile. Everything about him from his wide shoulders to his crooked nose and pillowy lips is designed to bring a woman down to her knees, seduce her until she's lost her mind. He's danger inviting you to play, and only a fool would accept his invitation, or, perhaps only a fool wouldn't.

"Yes, of course, I know her. She's with me," he replies in English again. Danger focuses on me, striking blue eyes against tan skin, and smirks before giving me a quick spank on the ass. "Right, beautiful?"

"Right." Blushing furiously, I throw daggers at him which makes him chuckle, his eyes dancing with amusement. "I'm sorry I was so late," I say, smiling sweetly at him then pinch his side, hard. I smile a real smile when he flinches, hiding his howl of pain behind a cough. *Gotcha.* "I hope you didn't miss me terribly, my love."

"I missed you so much *it hurt.*" A cheeky grin tilts the corner of his mouth when he palms my ass. Slowly. Leisurely. My eyes widen at his intimate, provoking touch, wiping the smile off of my face. This man is deranged. Yes, that's the only explanation for his behavior.

"Now if you'll excuse us, Margot, I need a minute alone with my little love," he says the last three words with barely contained laughter.

Margot appears confused at our interaction, her gaze bouncing from him to me and vice versa. She narrows her eyes, obviously not buying his story. Shaking her head, she rolls her eyes. "Whatever you say. Just see her out when you're done playing," she comments in English. *So the infuriating woman knew English after all.* And with that, she spins on her feet and leaves us, taking the two security guards with her. The circus over, the disappointed crowd disperses.

The stranger takes me by the forearm and makes me follow him to the back of the gallery where there isn't another soul besides the two of us.

"Are you crazy?" I twist my arm, freeing myself from his hold. Indignation makes me shake from head to toe. "Why would you do that?"

To add insult to injury, the maddening, gorgeous man seems to be enjoying himself. "Easy, beautiful. I think I just saved your neck back there."

"But—" *He has a point. Darn it.* "Thank you, but—"

"You're welcome," he adds cheekily, his mouth twitching.

"But you *kissed* me," I say, my pride still smarting at the way he handled me.

"You didn't seem to mind too much, *ma chérie.*" His lips curve dangerously as his heavy-lidded eyes fall upon my mouth first and then my eyes. "You kissed me right back."

My cheeks are on fire. The memories of his kiss, the heat and the strength of his arms around me, spin inside my head like a revolving door, leaving me dizzy. Flustered, I say, "You-you caught me off-guard. That's all."

"Sure, beautiful." He leans lazily on the wall, crossing his arms. He appears at ease and full of himself. "Besides I'll be damned if I have to apologize for kissing you."

He peels himself away from the wall and closes the space between us. My heart drums out of my chest. I know I should move, but my feet seem frozen on the spot, my fight or flight response rendered useless by a man with the devil in his eyes fast approaching me. He watches me as though I am already in his bed, naked, ready to be taken by him. And my God, for a weak, treacherous second, I wonder what it would be like. Animalistic. Feral. Erotic. Just like him.

When he's standing in front of me, he leans down until his lips are almost grazing mine. His breath, soft and sweet, against my skin. "Because I liked it. Very much. In fact, I'm tempted to kiss you again."

I take a step back, fear, and maybe excitement, running freely in my veins. "You wouldn't dare."

"You know I would, and you'd love it as much as the first time."

"You're ridiculous." I laugh in disbelief and shaken to the core. "I'm leaving now. Thanks for the rescue," I add sarcastically.

I don't wait for his answer. I turn blindly on my feet, leaving the man standing behind me. Every part of me begs to rush out of the gallery and put as much space as possible between us, but I force myself to slow down, each step deliberate and assured, showing him that he didn't get to me.

"Wait, that's the—" he adds, but I ignore him. Turns out to be a mistake because I find myself in some room rather than nearer to the exit door. Seriously? *Seriously?* I'm not prone to tantrums, but I'm very close to stamping my feet on the floor.

Blushing angrily, my hands in fists, I walk back only to find him standing languidly in the same spot where I left him. His eyes dance with mirth. "Made the wrong turn?"

"Go to hell."

The last thing I hear is his laughter.

CHAPTER THREE

The next day ...

AFTER A MORNING RUN, I stop outside the building to catch my breath. Sweat drips down my forehead and every muscle in my body burns, but I'm feeling good. I'm bent over at the waist with my hands on my knees when a couple bumps into me. They utter a quick, indifferent apology in French without glancing my way and disappear in the building. *Great, I guess I just met a neighbor.*

Sighing, I shake my head and follow suit. I check myself when I notice the same couple waiting for the elevator in the lobby. They're too occupied with one another to notice they're no longer alone. I can't see his face from this angle. Only hers. He pushes her back against the wall as the woman laughs throatily. Her laughter disappears as he begins to lazily kiss her while she holds onto his shoulders for support.

Unimpressed and beyond uncomfortable by their lack of tact, I put as much space between us as possible, and press the up button repeatedly. To distract myself, I stare at the marble floor and methodically count its black and white tiles.

Not that it works.

I can still hear the woman moaning softly between kisses as he whispers tantalizing words in her ear. I don't understand, but there's no need. Pleasure and maddening carnal desire vibrate through every syllable he utters, hypnotizing her. The thought of what he could be saying makes my cheeks grow warm.

I try not to look their way but curiosity, tempting as always, wins in the end. The couple is lost in their heated embrace, unaware of their surroundings. His face buried in her neck, my eyes focus on her hand, following its every move as she palms the outline of his back. The eroticism of it all hits me like a drug. A potent high. I want to look away, but I can't. William doesn't believe in public displays of affection such as this. He finds them distasteful and beneath himself and his name. He would never touch me like that outside the privacy of our bedroom, and I don't think I'd let him.

But part of me is fascinated. Captivated by the indecent scene unfolding in front of my eyes. And for a moment, I'm jealous of this man and woman who can easily give their middle finger to convention and the rules of etiquette in the name of lust and desire. Once upon a time, I didn't care what people thought of me. Freedom felt too good to give a shit. But that was many years and lifetimes ago. My errant mind drifts to last night, the indecent stranger, the damn kiss, and everything it made me feel, but I angrily shove those thoughts out of my head. Wishing I could exorcise the experience from my memory completely.

Trance-like, I accidentally drop my phone, and the sound of it landing on the tile floor catches the stranger's attention. At once he stops kissing her and looks in my direction. Surprise registers in his face. *This cannot be happening*, I think to myself. *This cannot be happening to me.* The ground beneath my feet shakes. I wish myself buried six feet under. Or back in the safety of my home in Greenwich. Because the eyes of the devil—the same vivid blue eyes I wished to never see again—are staring right into mine.

He lets go of the woman, runs his fingers through his raven hair, his movements easy and careless yet assured, and walks towards me. As he closes the short distance between us, I remain frozen like a statue. He bends down to pick up my forgotten phone and hands it back to me. An insolent half smile pulls the left corner of his mouth.

"Looks like fate has a macabre sense of humor."

"Thank you," I reply coolly, trying to hide the chaos raging inside me as we stare at each other. I reach for my phone, making sure not to touch him. "And yes, it appears that way."

His gaze on me feels as though he's undressing me with his eyes. "I thought I'd never see you again," he says softly, his words like a caress.

"Sébastien ... *mon amour,*" the attractive woman says, drawing his attention to her.

The elevator arrives. By the time the doors open, I'm grateful for the brief escape it offers. I step in, cross my arms, and proceed to focus all of my attention on the buttons, studying them as though they are the most interesting thing I've ever seen. And when they join me inside, I pretend they don't exist, yet I am keenly aware of him, of every move he makes, and his smell—like a forest in winter. Clean, crisp, woodsy.

Upon reaching my floor, I step out of the elevator as calmly as possible even though I feel like a pack of wolves is hot on my heels. I try not to look back, but I'm unable to stop myself from stealing one last glance of him—the biggest and most threatening wolf of all. It turns out to be a mistake. I find him staring back, appearing like he's ready to have me for his meal. He watches my face unabashedly. Taunting me. Inviting me. Reminding me of what happened between us.

"See you around, neighbor," he says, his words a promise. He smiles roguishly as he reaches for the girl's hand and places a kiss on her open palm that goes straight to my core.

Like a coward, I want to look away, but I won't let him see how deeply under my skin he's gotten.

"Don't count on it," I say, raising my chin and holding his gaze as the elevator doors close in front of us.

Later that day ...

Numb on the inside, I stare at the cream-colored tiles in front of me. "So you're not coming anymore?" I ask hollowly, gripping the phone tighter as I turn the stove off. The meat sauce bubbling in the large metal pot, William's favorite, is forgotten.

"What happened?" I step away from the kitchen, suddenly feeling sick by the smell of oregano and tomatoes.

"Larry needs me here, darling. A lot of money is on the line with this acquisition."

"What about your meetings here?"

23

"They've been moved to later in the year."

Two days ago, when William told me to come to Paris ahead of him because of a "last minute" rescheduling of his meetings, I should have known. But things were going great, and so I believed him. I thought we had turned over a new leaf. And if he was trying to work on us, the least he deserved was my trust.

As soon as I walked into the gorgeously decorated apartment, I threw myself body and soul into making it a home. I don't know how to do much, but I can create a mean flower arrangement and stock a fridge, and I'd kept myself busy, willing the hours away until William would finally arrive. *When everything would be as it should be.* And if a little voice whispered close to my ear that something was wrong, I've ignored it. This was the new us. The new us has no room for my old fears and paranoia.

"Of course it's not what I want," he says over the phone, pretending to be frustrated. I can almost picture him sitting in the leather chair of his office as he runs his fingers through his hair. "But my hands are tied. I'm needed here."

I take a deep breath and close my eyes, realizing that I'm fighting a losing battle. "There's no point talking about this anymore. The fact is I'm here, and you're there. And you're not coming anymore."

"Val—"

"Don't," I say a little too forcibly. Loosening the grip on the phone, I wipe a tear angrily off my face with the back of my hand. When I'm more in control of my stupid emotions, I add, "This is what I'm going to do—I'm going to stay here."

"You're not coming home?"

"No, I don't think I will." I suck in a breath, searching within me for strength to stand against him. "I need to be alone. I need time to think. Time to sort things out in my head. And I obviously can't do it around you." *Because I'm a fool around you.* He continues to feed me lies, and I continue to eat them, hungrily swallowing them, because I'm starving.

"For fuck's sake, Val. Sort *what* things out?"

I let out a sigh, going to the bathroom in search of a tissue to blow my nose. "Do you really have to ask?"

He's silent for a moment too long. It's deafening and final.

Suddenly tired, so tired, I sit on the floor of the bathroom, the cold of the tiles seeping into my bones, and lean back against the wall. I know I might be overreacting. It's just a trip, no? But I'm angry with myself for falling for his lies again, and I have no one else to blame for that but my weak heart.

"Let me ask you something. Did you mean any of the things you said? Or was it all bullshit?"

If he were standing in front of me, this is where he would look away, unable to meet my gaze. "Of course I meant it, Val. I still do."

So many thoughts embedded with doubts and fears run through my head. I hate it, but I can't stop them from overcrowding my mind. If what he's saying is true, then why doesn't he just fly here once those meetings are over? Take the time off he promised. Was the trip a ruse to get me out of his hair, out of the city? Is he fucking around again? However, I can't bring myself to voice any of them. I keep them to myself, rotting inside me. Because I'm weak, and I'm afraid to find out what the answers will be. Denial is such a luring, deceitful bitch, isn't it?

"Sometimes I wish I were strong enough to leave you." I pause, feeling hot streaks of tears falling diagonally on my skin, picturing his green eyes. "Maybe I'm a bigger fool than I originally thought because I can't stop myself from loving you."

I hang up the phone without giving him another chance to answer.

CHAPTER
FOUR

"Do you know what I thought when I first saw you?" William asked, pulling me closer to him.

The Pacific Ocean was our backdrop as we danced on the beach of Puerto Escondido. The restaurant where we had dinner was playing "El Lado Oscuro" by Jarabe de Palo. Mezcal was running freely in our veins. The sand in our feet. The salty, hot, humid air embraced our skin. The stars shone brightly. The sound of the waves crashing not far from us. I wanted to freeze time and make the moment last forever. I reclined my cheek on his chest and listened to the beating of his heart.

"No … you've never said."

"You were crying to Sailor about a guy."

"One of my finest moments," I said sarcastically.

"I found it endearing."

I groaned. "It was pathetic. But you were saying … What did you think about me?"

"Are you fishing for a compliment, Mrs. Fitzpatrick?"

"When am I not?"

He laughed, and the sound alone could drive a woman mad. I bit my lip to stop myself from moaning as he began to kiss my neck, my bare shoulder, every part of me he could reach. "I saw this girl, barely a woman. She had long, wild, curly hair. Her clothes didn't quite match. And she was talking so fast between sobs it was hard to keep up with what she was saying."

"Oh God." I buried my face in his chest. "That bad?"

He placed a finger under my chin and gently tilted my head up until our gazes met. "Yet every blue-blooded man in that coffee shop couldn't take his eyes off of her."

"Were you one?" I asked shyly, my heart beginning to drum a mad tattoo.

"Darling, I was jealous of the barista who got to serve you. I was jealous of the man who made you cry. I was jealous of every man who came before and would come after me. Someone offered you a napkin, trying to catch your attention. I watched him, ready to punch him for daring to go near you, but then you barely noticed him. You were so oblivious of your effect on men." He paused. "You still are."

"I've never cared about any of those things."

He smiled ruefully. "I know."

"Besides, I only care about one man." I stopped dancing and took his hands in mine. I lifted them to my mouth and kissed each of his palms. "I belong to you."

"I know."

The young waitress places a plate full of fruit and an espresso on the table. *"Merci."* I reach for the napkin and place it on my lap.

"De rien." She smiles before walking to the next table to take their order.

Not really hungry, I reach for the china cup. As my fingers grow warm with the heat coming from the cup, I take a deep breath and enjoy the smell of coffee filling my lungs.

It's funny how certain things remind me of William and our life together. Breakfast on the table. The smell of coffee. Mezcal. Spanish music. Every memory is embedded in me, part of who I am. If you had asked me the day I married him if I thought our marriage was strong enough to endure temptation, weakness, poverty, highs and lows, grief, losses—every damn proverbial curveball thrown at us—I would have laughed in your face and said that our love could survive it all. Funny thing is, I truly believed it. We were so happy. But then again, it had never crossed my mind that William would have an affair with another woman. Or lead a separate life with her behind my back. Sailor begged me to leave him.

But I couldn't.

I take a sip of the espresso, watching the Parisian people carrying on with their lives outside the café on streets full of history and beauty. My therapist asked me why I stayed—was it the money? The status? My cushiony lifestyle? Love? Memories of what we had been, what we were? Fear of the unknown, of being lonely and what I'd be throwing away? I wasn't a practical person. I always let my heart lead the way, but when faced with those questions and the stark reality they offered, it was hard to fool myself.

It wasn't only my love for William that made me stay. I had done nothing with my life except be William's wife, and the thought of figuring out who I was without him terrified me. It still does. If I'm honest with myself, I think that's what hurts the most about his betrayal. That he made a farce of everything I stood for, everything I held dear. He made me doubt myself as a wife, as a person, and as a woman.

Almost finished with my espresso, I browse a travel guide of Paris, unsure of where to go next. The Louvre or Notre Dame? After the phone call and a good cry, I'd made a pact with myself that I wouldn't let the state of my marriage bring me down or allow the turmoil inside me ruin my stay. *Screw that.* I won't give my husband the satisfaction to wreck this, too. I'm in Paris, the City of Light, where Picasso, Hemingway, Matisse, and many others lived. I plan on enjoying myself while figuring out what to do with my life and whatever is left of our marriage.

I push my glasses higher up my nose while reading a passage about the architecture of the famous Cathedral. William hates them, saying they make me look like a nerd. He would always ask me to not wear "those stupid things" and put my contacts in. I smile, pleased. I guess I still have a streak of rebellion left in me.

The waitress comes over to remove my plate. I'm thanking her when the maddening man from the gallery walks by the cafe, the one whose kiss and arms I still feel around me like phantom limbs. His gait is easy and relaxed. He's almost past the restaurant but stops when he recognizes an older gentleman sitting a few tables away from me. He goes to talk to him, and my heart goes into overdrive by his mere proximity. They shoot the breeze for a little. And like a Peeping Tom, I seem unable to stop watching him. The way his hair falls loosely over an eyebrow. This boyish half-smile that lingers after he laughs at something the other man said. The sharp lines of his features at odds with the lushness of his lips. Brutal. That's it. He's brutally handsome without even trying.

He looks up and lets his gaze travel across his surroundings. Panic, and fear that he'll notice or catch me gawking at him, makes me drop my book clumsily on my lap. With my heart in my throat, I pick it back up as fast as my awkward fingers will allow, raise and hide behind it, pretending to read while silently praying that he didn't see me.

Please. Please.

"Hello, neighbor."

Crap.

"Hey." I force myself to meet his eyes, and I'm taken aback once more by how piercing they are. They are eyes that make love and enslave you. But then again, everything about him is designed to awaken one's darkest, most erotic fantasies. "Hi. I didn't see you there."

If he knows I'm full of shit, he doesn't call me out on it. "How's the book?" He tilts his head to the right as though trying to read the title. The corners of his mouth twitch, amusement dancing in his eyes.

"The book? Oh, yes. Great." I glance at the culprit and notice I'm holding it upside down. *Oh, for fuck's sake.* I flip it back up. "I was trying ... you know. To look at a picture from all angles," I add lamely. *Seriously, Valentina? All angles?*

He chuckles, and the sound is throaty and masculine and spine tingling. "I keep bumping into you," he adds quietly, a soft, slow, and intoxicating smile lingering on that full mouth of his.

"Is that a good thing or bad?"

"I don't know ... I'm still trying to figure it out." He looks at the empty chair across the table from me. "May I?"

"No, I was—"

He pulls the chair out and sits down across from me, our knees touching. He takes off his leather jacket and drapes it over the back. While he does, I try my damn hardest not to gape at him. Wearing only a faded black tee that molds to his muscular chest, it takes every ounce of willpower I own to tear my gaze away from him and his golden skin.

"Getting ready to leave ..."

He nods towards the book lying open on the table. "Where you going?"

I shut it closed. "Nowhere."

"*Bien.*" He looks around for the waitress to place an order, but he might as well save himself the trouble. She's been eyeing him hungrily since he sat down, waiting for the chance to approach him. "Then you can join me for a glass of wine."

I grab my bag, preparing to leave. "I'd rather not, but thank you for the offer."

"You're still mad about the other day?" He reaches across the tiny table for my hand. "If so, I'm sorry."

"I thought you weren't going to apologize." The warmth of his touch sends a shot of electric heat running through me stirring my senses. However, logic, or self-preservation, wins and I remove my hand.

"I'm not. I'm sorry it upset you, but I'm not sorry it happened. Stay."

"As I've already said, I'd rather not." Everything about him makes me want to put an ocean between us.

He tilts his head to the side, sizing me up. "Pity ... I didn't peg you for a coward."

I tighten my grip on my bag, offended. "I'm not."

"Prove it." He raises an eyebrow. "Have a glass of wine with me."

Without saying a word, I let go of my bag and sit back down. I fold my hands primly over my lap and raise my eyes to meet his, responding silently to his challenge. *Well, two can most certainly tango.*

He grins approvingly.

The waitress comes over, and it seems for the time being we've reached a temporary truce. His gaze remains trained on me while he orders a bottle of Brunello, and I fight the urge to fidget in my seat. The waitress walks away, leaving us to ourselves.

Leaning back comfortably in the chair, he rests his leg horizontally over the knee of the other as he runs both of his hands through his longish jet-black hair. My fingers itch to touch its softness. "They suit you." He points toward my eyes.

Instinctively, my hands go to my round, horn-rimmed glasses, and I inwardly groan when I realize what he's referring to. I start to remove them but decide to keep them on.

"Good decision. I like them on you."

My heart skips a beat. I blush furiously. "Thanks," I say, but the statement comes out sounding more like a question.

"You're welcome." He watches me closely as his fingers gently brush the crest of my cheek. The contact makes me feel as though I'm being doused with gasoline and lit on fire. "You look lovely when you blush."

"Do you always speak whatever is on your mind?" I laugh

shakily as I curl my fingers around the espresso cup and drum them nervously on its surface, the smell of coffee and buttery croissants floating around us. The memory of his kiss and the reality of his touch pierce me like an arrow. "Do whatever you want?"

He chuckles. "Oui, you should give it a try someday."

"Is that why you kissed me?"

I flinch internally. *Why did I have to bring it up? Now, he's going to think I've been thinking about it.* Which I have, but he doesn't need to know that. *Damn it.*

"I kissed you because I wanted to."

"That's not a good reason to go around kissing strange women."

"Well, what was your reason for kissing me back?"

Touché.

I focus on the now-cold dark brew in between my hands, trying not to laugh at this impossible man. "Whatever happened to Margot?"

"She got over it, I'm sure."

"God, I hope so. She was really mad ... Not that I blame her, though."

"What made you go inside anyway?"

"Made a mistake. I didn't realize I was crashing a party until it was too late." I bite my lip, remembering the whole thing, finding it sort of funny now. "Actually, I was about to leave when I saw this painting with a poppy flower."

"Oh yeah? Bet you it was terrible."

"Not at all. Whoever painted it is very talented. You could see the love. Feel the pain."

"How?" he asks softly, the question almost a whisper.

"I know I'm not making sense, but something about the painting made me hurt for the artist. Call it fanciful, but I felt—I felt as though it was his heart on the canvas."

"That's fanciful all right." He clears his throat, a shadow clouding his eyes momentarily. He blinks, and it's gone. "So, neighbor. What brings you to Paris?"

"Call me Valentina, please." I take a deep breath, trying to think of an excuse. "Just needed a break, I guess."

"I'm Sébastien," he says with the most divine French accent. "A break from what?"

"Sébastien," I repeat, rolling the word on my tongue, tasting it. I don't understand why but my heart goes into overdrive by just saying his name out loud. "A break from life, I guess."

"You came to the right place. Did you travel alone?"

I nod. "My husband stayed behind in New York." At the mention of William, I'm assailed with guilt. Focusing on my hands, I think of excuses so I can leave.

"You know, if you keep staring at that table, you're going to burn a hole in it," he says good-humoredly.

I raise my eyes swiftly, meeting his.

"There." He stares at me as he crumbles my defenses little by little. His gaze takes me to a dark corner, undresses me, and fucks me. "That's better."

I should get up and walk away from him, but like the other night at the gallery, I find myself unable to move. I foolishly remain seated because I know, deep down, I don't want to leave. I want to stay with him next to me. It's a risky game to play, but I can't seem to make myself care.

"Don't look at me that way, please," I beg softly.

"Why not?" He reaches into the pocket of his jacket, pulling out a packet of cigarettes. At ease, he places one loosely between his lips, lighting it. He tilts his head back and blows smoke out of his mouth. "You're a beautiful woman."

And for a crazy, reckless instant, I wonder what it would be like to kiss him again. Would it be as good as the first time? Would he make me feel the same yearning? The same hunger? I tighten my hold on the cup, surprised it hasn't shattered between my hands as an intense need to touch him comes over me. "Because I like it, and I shouldn't."

"Because you're married?"

"Yes."

"What if I told you I don't care?" He licks his lower lip, the tip of his tongue tracing its pillowy outline, as he brings his hand up close to his mouth about to take another drag, stopping halfway. A slow, lethally attractive smile spreads across his face, the corner of his eyes crinkling. "What are you *really* afraid of, Valentina?"

You. Me. "I must go."

Before giving him a chance to protest, I grab my Birkin bag and get up, pushing the chair back and rushing out the door. I can still hear the bell on the door ringing as I pull my Burberry trench closer around me, walking as fast as my feet will take me.

Walking as far away as possible from that café, the man inside, and everything he makes me crave and desire.

The next day I'm coming home from a walk when I find a large parcel waiting outside my door. Frowning, my gaze lands on a note stuck under the string. I open it.

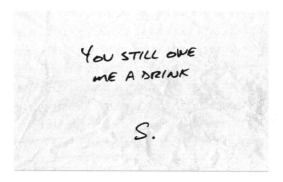

Nerves cause my hands to shake as I rip the paper off. Urgency makes my movements clumsy, which makes me take longer, and I gasp when I find the painting I admired the other night—the painting that led me to meet Sébastien. In a daze, I search for the signature and find it on the bottom right corner.

S. Leroux

Oh, my God.
It's him.

CHAPTER FIVE

"WHAT ARE YOU THINKING ABOUT?"

I leaned back on the headrest, enjoying the warm wind and hair whipping my face. It's one of the first days of spring. The sun is out, the flowers are blooming, and everyone has ditched their winter clothes for shorts and dresses. "I'm nervous."

William reached for my hand and laced our fingers together. "Don't be. My family is going to love you."

I looked at his flawless profile as he drove the car with the top down. "You're just saying that to calm my nerves."

"Of course I am."

I smacked him on the shoulder, making him laugh. "Asshole."

"Forgive me." He raised my hand to his lips and kissed it. "I know my family will love you because they only want what's best for me, and you are it, Val. Haven't you noticed? I'm crazy about you."

Smiling cheekily, a wild impulse came over me to discompose his perfect facade, perhaps drive him mad with want, tease him until he was at my mercy. "How crazy?" I asked as I guided my hand toward his hardness, running my fingers over his cock. "How crazy are you about me, William?" I asked throatily, feeling the bulge in his pants turn rock hard beneath my touch, listening to his breathing accelerate. "Enough to let me go down on you right now?"

"Val ..." he begged, his voice deepening with hunger.

I unbuckled myself, throwing caution to the wind, and kneeled on my

34

seat as I bent down, the gearshift digging in my ribs, and slowly unzipped his khaki pants. Out of the corner of my eye, I saw William tightening his grip on the steering wheel as color flooded the crests of his cheeks. I smiled, drugged with him and freedom. I didn't care that there were cars around us or that someone could easily see us out of their window. I took him in my mouth and his musky flavor and thickness filled me again and again. The sun on my skin, his taste on my tongue, recklessness ran through my veins, wetness gathered between my legs.

His chest rose with each breath. "I'm going to crash the car, woman."

I laughed, kissed the tip of his cock, and whispered in his ear, "Then pull over," I nipped his earlobe, "and fuck me."

I heard him curse before he pulled over to the side of the highway. I laughed as I removed my thong as fast as I could. He grabbed me by the waist and pulled me on top of him, impaling me in one deep thrust. It was fast. Hard. Needy. Indecent. The steering wheel dug in my back, my knees hitting the door and the gearshift. It didn't matter. We climaxed quickly and intensely and as one.

I knew William had been adopted by a family with a lot of money, his name alone told me so, but I couldn't give two fucks about it. I was in love with William. If anything, I found his wealth to be intimidating. Some of the gifts he'd given me in the past could probably feed a small nation.

But as the iron gates that protected his family estate opened to let us in, and we traveled on a winding road up a hill full of trees and rolling green grass, I couldn't help but wonder if I was in over my head. We had been dating for more than a year, and things were getting serious between us. Yet, as we approached the sprawling, majestic manor, I felt only panic and fear bubble inside me. What if his family didn't like me? What if they didn't think I'd be good enough for the heir of the family? I knew my worth, but as I stared at the huge house in front of me, I began to doubt whether I was the right woman for William.

I licked my dry lips, William's flavor still lingering on them, as I tried to smooth my simple, plain day dress. What did one wear to meet American Royalty? I pictured his grandmother and sister dressed in country club attire while I showed up wearing a puffy ball dress. I laughed.

"What's so funny?"

I turned to look at William, his blond hair messy from my hands, his lips swollen from my kisses, and I wondered if his smell remained on my body like the shadow of his touch.

"Nothing."

We stared at each other, and I saw all the love he felt for me. And that love gave me strength to face his family and whatever happened next.

We found his adoptive grandmother, his adoptive sister and her husband, and a friend of the family on the veranda having lunch al fresco. There were two large umbrellas shielding the guests from the sun. Crystal glasses brimmed with lemonade or champagne, and plates filled with every delicacy imaginable to man.

As soon as the matriarch of the family saw William, she smiled tenderly at him, pride and love shining in her eyes. She appeared to be in her late seventies, with perfectly coiffed ice-blond hair and porcelain white skin unmarred by the sun. Loretta reminded me of winter. When her eyes met mine, I felt like an errant child under her appraising gaze, and I knew she found me lacking and underserving of her grandson.

His sister, so very blond, so very tall and so very rich, inspected my dress, probably realizing right away that I had purchased it at a discount store two seasons ago. I tucked a strand of my unruly hair behind an ear, feeling like show cattle. William must have sensed my discomfort because he reached for my hand and gave it an encouraging squeeze.

"There you are, William. Come and give this old woman a kiss."

With my hand in his, William walked around the table to where she was sitting. He let go of me to bend down and kiss his grandmother on each cheek as she watched him closely. "I haven't seen you in a very long time. I thought you'd forgotten all about me."

"How could I forget my first love," he replied suavely.

"Oh, save your pretty words for someone else. They don't work with me," she said, appearing to enjoy his words nonetheless.

He straightened, smiling ruefully. "I've been busy. But I'm here now, and I've brought someone very special to me for you to meet. This is Valentina, Grandmother." He reached for me and brought me to stand in front of her. "And, Valentina, this is my grandmother Loretta."

I extended a hand, but she dismissed it. "Come, let me kiss you since you're my William's sweetheart."

William's sweetheart, she'd called me. And my heart was happy. But I should have known then that one day that's all I would be, and all I would become. Not Valentina, but William's sweetheart—his possession and nothing else. A person without an identity except for the one bestowed on her. I bent down, and as her lips landed on both of my cheeks, I felt an unwelcome chill spread throughout me.

"What about us, Will? Won't you introduce her to the rest of your family?" his sister teased.

He introduced me to his sister, Gwyneth; his brother-in-law, Christian, who was too busy drinking and eating his lunch to notice me; and Julie, a longtime friend of Gwyneth and William's.

As we sat down next to Julie, something about the way she looked at William gave me the idea that once upon a time they had been more than friends. Oddly enough I didn't feel any jealousy, but then again, I wasn't the jealous type.

"How was your drive?" Julie asked William, pretending I didn't exist.

"Bumpy." I placed a hand on his leg, my touch reminding him of what happened in the car less than an hour ago, and smiled at William as he started to choke on the champagne. "But uneventful."

Maybe I was the jealous type after all.

"Where are you from, Valentina?" Gwyneth asked with a sweetness that didn't quite reach her eyes.

"A town near Albany."

"Oh, really?" Gwyneth perked up. "Where exactly? We might have some acquaintances in common. My ex lives there, you know? He's the governor of New York." She laughed carelessly as she studied my face and attire down to my gently worn flats. "But then again, I doubt we run in the same circles."

"Gwyneth," William warned her. "I think you've had enough champagne."

"Julie, tell William to stop being such a fucking bore. I'm just trying to break the ice with—" She pointed toward me with a crystal flute full of champagne. "What did your say your name was? It's hard to keep up with William and all of his gol—"

"Gwyneth! That's enough," William said firmly.

Her words hit me like a bucket of freezing cold water. I wasn't expecting a warm welcome, but this hurt, especially coming from William's sister.

"Let's go, my love, I'd like to show you the rest of the house." He looked at Gwyneth as though she was the dirt beneath his shoe. "I'll deal with you later."

She pretended to shiver. "Oh, I'm shaking." She focused on her husband. "I'm bored, Christian. Take me home."

William placed his hand on the small of my back prompting me to follow him. Too stunned to think, I took a few steps blindly until I realized that if I walked away now, if I didn't stand my ground, she would win. And I wasn't going to allow that to happen. Not now, not ever.

I walked back to the table and stood in front of all of them. I took in *their expensive clothes, the air of arrogance imbedded in their features, and raised my chin proudly. "You're right. You and I don't run in the same circles. I grew up in a trailer in an area of Albany that you'd probably think beneath you. My father and mother were drug addicts who died of an overdose when I was barely three." I clenched my hands to stop myself from shaking. "My aunt raised me as her daughter while trying to support us on a waitressing job. I love her, and I'll never be ashamed of that no matter how you look at me or what you say.*

"I have no money and no fine name like yours, but I'm damn proud of what I've accomplished. I finished high school at the top of my class, and now I'm attending my dream college on a full scholarship. So, you can sit there judging me all you want, but I'll say it again, I'll never be ashamed of who I am and where I come from." I focused on William and his green gaze. "I love your brother. And I would continue to love him even if his name was John Smith."

"I've changed my mind, William." The grandmother watched me approvingly, a curious light in her eyes. "I like her. She's got spirit. You've done well for yourself, my darling boy."

"I know," William said, taking my hand. "Now if you'll excuse us."

I followed him silently inside the house. He guided us to a bedroom on the second floor and shut the door behind us. Before I knew what was happening, my back was flat against the wall and his lips were devouring mine. When we came up for air, he cupped my face gently in his hands. "I love you, Val."

"What?" I asked weakly. "What did you say?"

"I love you."

A sob escaped my lips as I grabbed him by the shirt and began to cry on his chest. "I-I thought you we-were going to break up with me," I cried. He laughed throatily making me punch him in the arm. "It's not funny you big brute of a man."

"I love you, my crazy, wild, beautiful Valentina." William wrapped his arms around me, pulling me in for a hug that left me breathless, and kissed my tears away one by one. "Will you marry me?"

My heart stopped beating as a starburst of emotions exploded inside me. Happiness. Awe. Disbelief. Love. "But what about your family? They won't be happy with this."

"I don't care about them."

"I don't know, William. I don't fit in your world. We're too different."

"How?"

"Look at you … Look at me."

"I am looking at you. Trust me, darling. You're all I see, all I want. Do you love me, Valentina?"

I kissed his chest, right where his heart was. "Of course, I do."

He kissed me thoroughly, making me forget about all of the reasons why it wouldn't work. "Then say yes, Valentina. I won't let anyone ever hurt you."

"Promise me?" I hated the fear I heard in my voice, but I couldn't believe this was actually happening to me.

"Yes, my love. I promise."

Many years later, he broke the one promise that mattered to me the most.

I toss and turn, burying my head under the pillow, but it won't work. I can still hear the music coming from the apartment above me. I reach for my phone on the nightstand and peek at the time. It's past eleven, for goodness sake. Groaning, I lie back down and stare at the ceiling as I consider calling the police. However, I dismiss the thought as quickly as it comes. I wouldn't even know what number to call. I close my eyes while covering my ears as a poor excuse to tune out all the noise. And like the pillow, it doesn't help at all.

Wide awake now, I give up all pretenses of sleep and spend the next few minutes watching the vibrations of the bass shake the crystal chandelier. *Thump. Thump. Thump. Thump. Thump. Thump. Thump. Thump. Thump. Thump. Thump.*

Enough.

I shove the duvet to the side, get out of bed, grab my cashmere cardigan, and go in search of whoever is blasting the music, ready to give them a piece of my mind. I don't even care that I barely know enough French to order food, let alone make a complaint to a neighbor. I'm sure I'll manage. *The musique is too fucking loud, vous understand?* I'm angry. Tired. And completely sober.

I skip the elevator, going for the stairs instead, and I am now standing outside the offending apartment. I pull my cardigan tighter around me as though it is armor and I am off to war. Lifting a hand, I knock a little too forcibly. For the few moments it takes the person to open the door, I try to picture who it could be on the other side. Maybe it's a kid having a party while his parents are away or an older person who can't hear too well. With that thought in mind, I mellow down a little.

The last person I expect to open the door is Sébastien. I swallow hard, my eyes widening. A very naked Sébastien. *My God, you're beautiful.*

He smirks cockily, trying not to laugh. "Thank you."

Oh, God. Please don't let me have said that out loud. Please. Please. "I said that out loud, didn't I?"

"Yes."

Figures.

I clear my throat uncomfortably, changing the subject. "You're not wearing a shirt."

His gaze along with mine slides down his naked torso, following the exposed muscles of his solid chest. Streaks of paint in different colors cover his right pectoral and some of the grooves of his six-pack. *He's breathtaking.* Blushing as though I'm showering in fire, I bite my lip and ball my hands into fists to stop myself from reaching out and tracing the perfect, deeply carved V between his hip bones or the happy trail disappearing under the waistband of his jeans. Everything about him from his gorgeous arms to the perfect thick grooves and muscles of his golden chest screams man, man, man. All fucking man. Forget about fallen angels. He's the King of the Underworld showing you how magnificent, how exquisite it would be to sin with him. An image flashes in my mind of me on my knees, a willing slave at his feet, while my mouth, my tongue, my fingers explore every wicked part of him. I catch the direction my thoughts are going and blush even more.

Smiling a slow, intoxicating smile, his eyes come back to meet mine. "Yes, it appears that I'm not." He places his forearm on the door, lazily leaning on it. "May I help you with something, Valentina?"

The way he says my name sends a delicious chill running down my spine. I suck in a breath, shaking my head. *Get your act together, woman. What are you? Seventeen?*

"I can't sleep."

He leans forward ever so slightly, and I swear I can feel the heat emanating from his body. "I can think of a few very entertaining ways to help you with that," he says, his voice inviting, his gaze flat out wicked.

"Yes, I mean," I stammer, cursing my clumsiness. "No, no, that's not what I meant. Your music. It's keeping me awake. I was wondering if you could turn it down a little, please."

"It depends."

I frown. "On what?"

He licks his lips. "What you're willing to give me in exchange."

I raise my eyebrows as my heart skips a beat. "You're kidding, right?"

He leans forward until his lips are close to my mouth. Until his sweet breath that smells like wine and cigarettes kisses my lips. "Not when it comes to you."

At that exact moment, we both hear a woman say, *"Bonsoir, Sébastien."*

I take a step back, shivering as Sébastien focuses his attention on the neighbor. *"Bonsoir, Marion. Vous passez une bonne soirée?"*

As the woman replies to Sébastien, he places his hand on the small of my back, the contact electrifying, and pulls me toward him. "Come with me," he whispers in my ear.

He addresses his neighbor once again, saying something that makes her laugh as he guides us both inside his apartment.

"Better wait in here or she'll be inviting herself for a nightcap," he adds as an explanation, smirking. When he leans forward, I think he's going to touch me. I suck in my breath and shrink back. Instead, he reaches for the handle and closes the door behind me not once coming into contact with me. "Don't be afraid of me, Valentina," he whispers huskily close to my ear, sending a shiver running down my spine.

I cross my arms, pulling the cardigan tighter about me. "I'm not."

The infuriating man smirks knowingly in return. I run a hand through my hair, thinking of a different topic, when I spot a painting hanging over his fireplace. "I haven't had a chance to properly thank you for your gift, so thank you. Why didn't you tell me it was you who painted it?"

"Didn't think it was important. Besides, now you know," he adds dismissively.

I disagree with him, but I drop the subject, an instinct telling me that he doesn't want to talk about it. With nothing else to discuss my mind yells at me to get out of here and go back to the safety of my apartment, but his warning about the neighbor stops me in my tracks. Seems like I'm stuck for the time being.

As a distraction, I stare nervously at everything but the man standing in front of me. His walls full of paintings. A welcoming living room. The kitchen to the left. The leather jacket that I recognize from yesterday thrown carelessly over the couch. The place looks warm, inviting, and lived in. It's all for nothing, though. A losing battle. Because every atom in my body is aware of him, attuned to him. I know when he rubs his face with his hands. I can smell the cigarette he just smoked. I can almost feel the sigh escaping his lips against my skin.

Meanwhile, time is taking its sweet slow ass time. Seconds seem like minutes and minutes seem like hours. When I've had enough, I break the silence. Well, technically speaking, both of us do. At the same time. Figures. Why not make this more uncomfortable than it already is.

"Would you like to—"

"I better—"

I bite my lip, fighting a smile from escaping. "You go first."

"No, you go ahead. What were you going to say?"

"I better go. It's getting late. Your turn. What were you going to say?"

A rueful smile touches his lips. "Nothing of importance. I'll take care of the music."

Music? What music? "Thank you." I reach for the handle and open the door, suddenly feeling like a deflating balloon because he didn't ... *Didn't what? Ask me to stay?* I shake my head. Sleep. Yes, that's what I need. Stepping out, I glance over my shoulder. "Good night."

"My offer still stands, by the way."

I stop walking and turn around to face him once more. "What offer?" I frown.

"That little problem about your sleep," he says, grinning wide like a little boy in a toy store.

"Good night, Sébastien." I roll my eyes, which makes him laugh. "Also, put a shirt on, won't you?"

A chuckle rumbles out. "*Bonne nuit*, Valentina."

On my way back to the apartment, I lift a hand to trace my lips and realize that I'm smiling.

CHAPTER SIX

WILLIAM IS ON TOP of me as we make out on my bed, the room in complete darkness. I can't see his face, but I can taste his saliva as his tongue wars with mine. His body melting with mine.

In the stillness of the night, my heart beats only for him and for the pleasure he brings me with his generous touch. Our heavy breathing and the rustling of our clothes break the silence surrounding us. His large frame weighs me down, holding me hostage to the sweet manipulation of my body, and I don't care. I love it all: the pressure, the hardness, the contact, the burn from within, and the yearning for more. He knows exactly how to touch me, how to tear aching moans from my chest as he laughs in my ear.

His lips are sucking on my neck as he dips his hand inside my underwear, spreading me open, his fingers rubbing me awake. His invasion grows faster, harder, yet it's not enough. I begin to fuck myself against his fingers now deep inside me, grinding myself against them. Begging him with my body to never stop. I want him to ease the ache between my legs yet continue to torment me. The precision with which he strokes me and plays with my clit makes me lose control.

The roots of my hair are wet with sweat. My breasts in my hands, rubbing myself. The smell of sex around us. Trembling, my moans are getting louder and louder as he drives me closer to sweet oblivion. His mouth on mine, kissing me with such starvation it feels as though he's sucking all the oxygen out of my lungs. His lips fuck me kiss by kiss as his hand fucks me thrust by thrust, rendering my mind and body useless. And all I can do, all I'm capable of, is to feel. Feel. Feel. Feel. Nothing but feel. Lust flows freely in my veins. Need making me spread my legs wider for him, wantonly offering myself to him. Welcoming him, begging him to take me. And he takes me so damn good. Open mouthed, our tongues tangle becoming one. I hold his wide shoulders slippery from sweat as he loses all restraint, finger fucking me to heaven. And then I come apart, my body shattering on the white sheets of our bed.

Seconds pass by as our breathing slows down. In the darkness, William's features remain hidden, but I can feel his weight pressing me down.

I sigh contentedly. "Mmm ..."

He laughs in my ear, his hot breath tickling my neck.

"Valentina ..." he whispers roughly, but the voice doesn't belong to William. It's Sebastien's voice that wakes me up from my dream, plunging me straight into reality.

Opening my eyes, I look around me, half fearing, half expecting to find Sébastien lying down on the bed next to me. Total silence and an empty room greet my eyes. Breathing heavily, shame spreads like black ink in my chest because for one moment, one weak second, before I woke up, I wished it were not a dream.

CHAPTER
SEVEN

I SPEND MY MORNING in Champs-Élysées. My French still sucks, but at least I can find my way without the help of a map or Pierre. I explore its stores and museums. Fall in love with the city and its magical je ne se quois. I stop at a charming bakery and have pistachio and vanilla macarons for lunch because why not. Life is too short to spend it hungry.

When I finally make it to the Arc de Triomphe, I brave the crowds of tourists like me, climbing all the way to the top. Upon reaching it, I gasp as my eyes take in the view of the whole city. There are tree-lined boulevards to my left and to my right. The Eiffel Tower stands outrageously tall and proud like a queen holding court amongst its subjects.

There's so much beauty around me that I didn't see before. And it's funny because, before this trip, all my memories of Paris were about William.

I close my eyes, enjoying the strong wind whipping my face. Five years ago, William brought me to Paris as a surprise after we'd got into a huge fight. We left New York with the ugly memory of it still ringing in our ears and resentment in our chests. However as soon as we arrived here, away from our problems, stripped from everyday life and everything that came with it, we were swept away by the magic the city had to offer. We weren't William and

Valentina anymore. We were just two old lovers rediscovering one another once again.

I saw the city through William's eyes, and it was enough. We went to the places he wanted to visit, ate the food he liked to eat, drank the wine he enjoyed, admired art he wished to see. I was happy because he was happy. Because I got to spend time with him. Time that was already rare, and, therefore, precious to me.

By then, longer hours at work and weekly business trips kept him away from me. Sometimes days would pass, and the only interaction we would share was a quick morning kiss and goodbye or a rushed call between meetings. I found ways to keep myself busy, to fill the void his absence created. Spin classes. Luncheons. Organizing benefits. I learned about wife bonuses over high-priced salads. I shopped for things I didn't need nor want, filling our house that felt more like a luxurious jail than a home. It was all a glittery front.

I knew I was very lucky. I had a roof over my head. A handsome husband. More money than I could ever spend in a lifetime. But did it matter when all I wanted was him?

Sometimes late at night, alone and tipsy with a glass of wine in hand while sneaking a cigarette on the balcony, I would wonder where I'd be had I not married William. What would my life be like if I hadn't called him? Maybe I would have run away with that guy from my Lit class. It wasn't disloyalty. It was curiosity. Loneliness. Melancholy. And maybe too much wine. I would laugh then, but it would come out more like a sob, the pain too close to the surface and impossible to hide.

I started avoiding Sailor too. Sailor with the husband who had a 9 to 5 job that didn't pay him well enough. Sailor with the husband who adored her and their two young daughters. Sailor who always looked like a lovely mess with black bags under her eyes, traces of baby food dried on her inexpensive sweater, yet couldn't be happier or more in love. I fooled myself into thinking that we were drifting apart because our worlds were too different and we didn't have anything in common anymore.

But the truth is that I am jealous of her. So very jealous. I want what she has. I envy her small home with the ever-present smell of apple pie and vanilla. I want William to be there for me as Tucker is there for her, to look at me as he looks at her.

When I watched her feeding their daughter with her own body in the shabby living room as my empty hands felt my empty womb, the despair, the envy bordering on dislike, maybe even the hate I felt, became increasingly harder to hide or to ignore. I would go home and wait on the bed with the lights turned off for William to arrive. And when he finally walked through the doors of our bedroom, he'd kiss me on the cheek as he told me that he was exhausted. He'd ask me about my day without really caring what I had to say, thoughts of a shower and sleep already occupying his mind. And while he removed his tie, I would bring up the same topic I always did after visiting Sailor.

William, baby … I want to start a family.

His hand would freeze as his eyes met mine. *Again, Val? We've spoken about this before. We're young. We have a lifetime ahead of us. Why not wait a little longer? Enjoy each other.*

But I don't want to wait anymore. I've waited long enough.

Right now is not the best time, my love.

When will be the best time for you, William? It seems like it never is.

He would sigh, shaking his head. *I can't do this now. I've had a long day. Let's talk about it tomorrow.*

Yet tomorrow would never come. And the subject would be dropped like always. Maybe I should have seen it then. The first signs that all was not well, the small cracks that would eventually become fractures separating us. But I chose to live in the dark, because the dark was safe and it hid the truth and gave me temporary happiness.

I open my eyes, taking a deep breath. Paris looks very different to me now as I relearn it without William by my side. A little voice inside my head tells me that maybe it's not the city I'm relearning, but myself.

On my way back to the apartment, I stop outside a small, quaint flower shop with a blue front to admire the arrangements displayed in the window. Frowning, I take a step closer to the glass. Something about these flowers tugs at my heart. Maybe it's the way the rose petals are drooping like tired shoulders, or the dust muting the clarity of some of the vases. They remind me of neglected toys, the kind that once upon a time brought great pleasure to a child, but then she grew up, and now they sit forgotten in the corner of an attic.

When I'm about to go inside, I see an older gentleman standing behind the glass counter cleaning its surface listlessly. Desolately. His shoulders, like the roses on the window, are stooped, and his white hair messy as though it hasn't seen a comb in weeks. His eyes seem to be focused on his wrinkled hand and the worn-out cloth beneath it, but even from afar, I can tell his mind is somewhere else.

I open the door, hearing the bell announcing my presence. He looks up, his weathered gray eyes taking me in. I smile shyly, pressing my handbag closer to me. *"Bonjour."*

The gentleman nods without bothering to smile back before returning his attention to the counter once more, wiping away an imaginary spot. Dismissed, I walk hesitantly around the outdated place, observing the different blooms. Roses in different colors. Orchids in jade green vases. Carnations. Daffodils. Freesias. There aren't that many, and whatever is left seems to be dying along with the store. Sadness fills me from within as I steal a quick glance of the older man with the melancholic eyes. Store, man, and flowers alike seem to be wilting with time and the blues.

I return my attention to the flower in front of me. Extending a hand, I stroke the petals of a white orchid. "Hello, pretty thing."

Ever since I can remember, flowers have always been a big part of who I am. When I was little, I would spend hours in the small patch of wild grass behind the trailer. Lying on the ground, hands behind my head, I'd pretend to be Alice in Wonderland. And like in the Disney film, the few wildflowers that surrounded me would come alive and talk to me and sing along with me. My aunt used to shake her head at me calling me a silly chit, but some nights, after a good day of tips at the diner, I would find one of our kitchen glasses sitting on my nightstand filled with whatever flower was on sale. I would take care of them, and in return, they filled our home with color and beauty.

The old man coughs behind me, reminding me that I'm not alone. Blushing, I reach for the orchid and make my way to the counter. *What must he think of me?*

"Magnifique," I say, placing the flower on the table, proud of myself for not butchering the French language altogether. He wraps the orchid in cellophane and puts it in a brown paper bag as I reach for my wallet inside my bag, pulling out a credit card and handing it to him.

"Merci." He takes it and rings me up.

As he's swiping it in the machine, I inspect the rest of the store. The path to the back room is filled with discarded boxes. Dusty books pile up on the floor like tiny mountains, and the cheese and bread he had for lunch sit half eaten on a wooden table, a small fly buzzing around it. My gaze stops on a single frame hung on the wall behind the counter—the only thing that seems to be clear of dust in a place covered in it. Drawn to it, I study the aged black and white photograph of a young couple from afar. The handsome man in the picture is lazily reclining against the side of a car, his attention on the beautiful woman smiling for the camera. It's a gorgeous shot, but what truly makes it breathtaking is the emotion in the man's gaze. You can see his heart in his eyes, and his heart belongs to her. How he must have loved her.

There's a pang in my soul as sorrow spreads through my blood. I once dreamed to be loved like that, and, for a while, I thought my dream had come true.

But it turns out dreams don't last forever.

The gentleman finishes the transaction and hands me the receipt to sign. As I slide it back, my gaze lands on him standing directly underneath the picture and suddenly understanding dawns on me. I see it all too clear. The lack of warmth or a female touch. The dying flowers. The state of neglect in the store. But especially the man's empty eyes, so different from the photograph.

The man has lost his heart.

The transaction finished, all that there is left for me to do is to grab the bag with the orchid and take my leave. Part of me wants to linger in the store, keeping the lonely man company, but he would probably think I'm a psycho hanging around while talking to flowers.

I let out a resigned sigh, thank him, and walk out the door. When I've taken no more than five steps, I stop and take one last look at the man in the shop. He's gone back to polishing the same spot on the counter, his movements lifeless and colorless like his surroundings. I shake my head irritated at being so powerless. About to move, my eyes land on a handwritten ad Scotch-taped onto the window glass. I step closer to the window, take out my phone and type in the words in a translation app.

Recrute vendeur H/F

Oh, my God. *This is it.*

Energy jolts my senses like an electroshock. Acting on an impulse, I go back inside, tear the paper off the window and bring it with me to the counter. *What are you doing,* I hear a small voice inside me ask. *He doesn't want your help.* Well, he's stuck with it. *You have no experience other than a few floral design classes. When was the last time you even had a job? You're nothing but a pretty accessory.* That makes me pause. The old doubts come back like an angry wave, threatening to drag me back in its undertow. But there's another voice inside my head, growing louder and louder by the second. It tells me to keep walking, to not give up, to keep swimming.

You won't drown, Valentina.

You are strong enough.

Surprise registers in the man's expression when he sees me standing in front of him for the second time in a day. Butterflies wreck my stomach. I place the bag and ad on the counter. His gray eyes widen in astonishment as they land on the cream-colored sheet.

I reach for my bag and pull out my phone and a notepad. Opening the translation app, I type in:

Is the position still available?
Est ce que le poste est encore disponible?

I feel sheepish and a little silly, aware that the translation isn't always exact, but for now, it will have to do. This French is better than no French at all. After writing it on the notepad, I slide it across the glass toward him. The gentleman cracks a tiny smile as he scans the words written on the sheet, and in that brief second, he's the young man in the picture once again. A glimmer of hope lights me from the inside out because maybe I can help him after all. And the fact that I put that smile on his face fills me with a new sense of pride and joy—of purpose.

He raises his head and meets my eyes. And in that moment, it's as though we both see and recognize something in one another. Pain, maybe? Two souls shouting for help?

Biting my lip nervously, I point at the notepad first. *"Vendeur."* I point at myself then. "Me. *Moi.*"

He nods in understanding. Reaches for a pen and writes his response down. As I watch the blank ink marking the paper, I swear I can hear the beating of my heart. Feel it beating out of my chest.

The realization that I need this like I need my next breath hits me in the head like a brick.

I reach for the notepad with trembling fingers. When I read the one sentence, there's a burst of emotions in my chest—an explosion of bright colors—charging me with life.

Oui, le poste est toujours disponible. Vous êtes embauchée.

I look up the translation on my phone just to make sure that I'm not jumping to conclusions. The words begin to blur, and I realize that I'm crying tears of what? Joy? Exaltation? Yes and yes. Yes to everything.

I know it's silly. All I would be doing is helping a man lost in a decaying store, but to me, it means so much more.

It's something akin to freedom.

To independence.

I wipe my tears while laughing as the gentleman stares at me with a funny look on his face. On a whim, I lean over the counter and kiss him on each cheek, getting another chuckle and smile out of him. "Thank you, thank you ... I mean, merci. Merci."

He must think I'm a whack job. He gives a girl a job, and she starts to cry then proceeds to kiss him? Yeah, total basket case if you ask me. But if he only knew what he's doing for me—the precious gift he's giving me—the opportunity to do something as Valentina.

To *be* Valentina.

CHAPTER
EIGHT

I GOT A JOB.

Feeling high and happy, I want to break into a dance. I might be just helping a man at his decaying flower shop, but it means everything to me. I think of my life and what I've done since I married William. I finished college, and while my friends were applying for jobs, I was looking at a list of caterers for our wedding. Being William's wife used to be enough for me, more than enough really, but it isn't anymore.

After Mr. Lemaire and I manage to introduce ourselves with the help of hand gestures and the translator on my phone, we say goodbye. I'm supposed to start on Tuesday, four days from now, because he's going to visit his daughter over the weekend. *I think.* Please, translator, don't mess this up.

I'm walking into the building, my hands full of paper bags with groceries and the orchid, when I see Sébastien standing by the elevator, his attention arrested on his phone.

"Oh, it's you again." I stop momentarily as my heart skips a beat at the sight of him. My thirsty eyes drink him in as the memory of what I willed him to do to me while dreaming of him flashes in the recesses of my mind.

He looks up, our eyes meeting. "Nice to see you, too."

I bite my lip, dismayed at my behavior. "I'm sorry. That was *very* rude of me."

"No, you're not." He puts his phone away in the back pocket

of his jeans. Shakes his head as a teasing smile tugs the corners of his mouth. "Admit it."

Abashed, I laugh shakily. "I would never."

"Well, I, for one, can't complain." His gaze on me is like a defibrillator to the heart. Blushing, I press the bags closer to my chest. We stand in uncomfortable silence. I wish I were anywhere else but here, standing next to a man who makes me feel as though I'm drowning and flying at the same time. But even that lie sounds empty to my ears. Because if I'm honest with myself, there's no place I'd rather be.

He breaks the silence first when he moves toward me. "Here, let me help you with those."

"No, thank you." I sober up and take a step back, holding onto the bags as though they are the most precious cargo in the world. "I can carry them just fine."

"I'm sure you can, Valentina. But I'd like to help you nonetheless."

We remain standing there for what seems like a slow eternity. I can almost picture us. A woman unwilling to let go. A man offering help that she's terrified to accept. We fight over bags filled with food, but somehow it feels like more than that. And I'm afraid he knows it, too.

Yet ...

Yet my shoulders hurt, my arms hurt, my heart hurts. Would it be so terrible to let someone help me? To selfishly share my burden with him even if it is for a short while?

"Thank you," I say, nodding once. "Please be careful with the orchid."

"Sure."

Slowly and gently as though he's afraid I'll change my mind halfway, he takes the bags away from me, and I let him. It's nothing but politeness from his part yet it's everything. And when our hands touch, I don't remove mine right away. I keep them there, relishing the heat of his skin against mine. It's a brief moment that couldn't have lasted more than mere seconds. A simple touch between friends to the casual observer. Yet as we ride the elevator in silence, the ghost of his touch burning my skin, I sense an invisible bond forming between us that wasn't there before.

"I see you managed to find a shirt."

He grins. "Still thinking about it, eh?"

I laugh. "In your dreams, buddy."

"If you only knew." He winks, appearing like the perfect rogue he is.

A small smile on my lips, I want to say something else, but my mind draws a blank. Instead, I focus on the carpet beneath our feet. Its color and texture: green and furry.

"What are you thinking about?" he asks quietly.

I look up, meeting his blue, blue eyes. How easy it would be to drown, to be lost in them. "Nothing really." *You make me happy.* "You?"

"Can't tell you," he says good-humoredly. "Sorry."

"Hey—"

"Nope."

"But—"

We hear a ping and the very inopportune elevator doors open on my floor. We get out forced to drop the subject. Sébastien walks me to the front of my apartment where I take both paper bags from him and balance them on my hip. I extend my arm to shake hands with him, but he doesn't take my hand. Instead, I watch as he reaches into the pocket of his leather jacket, pulls out a small package wrapped in brown paper, and places it in my palm.

I frown. "What's this?"

"A gift, Valentina."

"You got me something?" I ask foolishly, unable to hide the pleasure bursting inside the cavities of my chest.

He nods, grinning. "It would appear so."

"You didn't have to."

He buries his hands in the back pockets of his jeans and shrugs. "I wanted to."

I stare at him, at the gift, touched beyond words by the gesture. "Thank you."

He grins boyishly. "Don't mention it."

Without letting go of his gift, I put the groceries on the floor. "May I?" I ask when I'm free to open the package. Curiosity and excitement make my fingers tremble slightly. He nods, expectation shining in his eyes.

I try to slow down the process of tearing the paper away so I don't appear too overeager in front of him. I take my time removing the ribbon and the tape even though I'm dying to find out what's inside.

"Are you always this thorough when opening a gift?" he asks, laughter coating in his voice.

"No." I chuckle. "But I'm trying really hard to behave with some kind of decorum fit for my age."

"Here, let me do it. Or we'll be here all day."

"Hey!" I say with mock outrage, but I let him take the box anyway. And if his fingers come into contact with mine as he removes the present from my hands, I pretend I don't notice.

He unwraps it in no time and gives it back to me, winking. "See, it wasn't so hard."

Smiling, I roll my eyes at him before focusing on the box once again. I open the lid and find inside a gorgeously carved wooden owl. "It's beautiful," I whisper. I trace the intricate and delicate design with my fingertips, its smooth grooves indenting my skin.

"You like it?"

"Yes," I nod, swallowing past the knot in my throat as I find his gaze waiting for mine. "I like it very much."

"Good." He rubs the back of his neck. "It reminded me of you."

"Thank you … I think." I can't help but smile. Being compared to a bird should hurt my vanity. However, the way he's looking at me makes me feel as though I'm the most beautiful woman he's ever seen.

"You know, I'd buy every owl in Paris to see you smile at me again like that," he murmurs.

My cheeks on fire, I stare at Sébastien, trapped by him. Taking in his obscene beauty and, perhaps for the first time, seeing past it. It's only human to be attracted to him, to take one look at him and wonder what if.

But there have been other attractive men before him who have flirted with me and not once have they ever come close to affecting me the way he does. It's not love. It isn't purely lust either. It's *him*. He's a balm, a soothing balm. Whenever he's near me, I'm not so alone or sad anymore. He angers me, but then he says something that makes me want to laugh. He unnerves me, yet I can stand next to him in silence and discover the peaceful music in it.

He places his hand on the door next to my head and leans forward until our mouths are almost touching. He smiles. But it isn't the smooth, practiced smile from before. This time it feels unrehearsed. Natural. And it is more lethal than the purest poison ever created. "I think this is where I kiss you, *ma petite chouette*."

"*Petite chouette?*"

"Little owl." Slowly, he raises a hand to gently push my glasses back into place.

It would be so easy to move an inch, to close the space between us and finally feel his lips on mine again. Learn his taste. Savor his kisses. Find out whether he's real or just a figment of my imagination. Lose myself in a brief, frenzied moment that offers me reprieve from reality. Wave a white flag in the losing battle that is Sébastien.

I do none of those things.

Instead, I laugh when I want to cry. "No. This is where I say thank you again and bid you a good night."

Breaking his gaze, I unlock the apartment, grab the bags, and step inside. Before I close the door, I turn to steal one last glance of him. "Thank you very much for the lovely gift. Good night, Sébastien."

"Wait. Before, in the elevator, you asked me what I was thinking."

"Yes?"

"Not much gets to me, Valentina. Quite the contrary, as a matter of fact. But back there ... a novel thing happened to me." The corners of his mouth quirk in an amused smile.

My heartbeat accelerates. "What's that?"

Eyes on me, he starts to walk backward toward the elevator. "I realized, maybe for the first time, what it feels like to want, to *need* something you cannot have." Upon reaching it, he presses its button. The elevator opens almost immediately in front of him. He places a hand on one side of the door, stopping it from closing. "And, *also*, for the first time in what hasn't been a short life, I find myself jealous of another man. It's quite humbling, actually." He laughs wryly. "And I don't think I like it one bit." He pauses. "Your husband is a very lucky man."

He gets in the elevator, leaving me all alone and missing his warmth. I close the door behind me. Lean on it and press a hand to my chest, feeling the mad beating of my heart. I realize I'm still holding the owl in my hand. Feeling a rush of *everything*, I raise it, bringing it to my lips, and kiss it.

CHAPTER NINE

Seconds pass without another message. My fingers hover on the screen, ready to reply as though I were a Pavlovian dog at the sound of the bell. However, I can't bring myself to do it. Call it pride or spitefulness, but something inside me forbids it. Then, I remind myself that I'm an adult, so I type back.

Valentina: Entertaining. I went to the Louvre. Got to see the Mona Lisa at last. The thought that I should tell William about Mr. Lemaire crosses my mind, but I choose not to.

William: Good. What are your plans for tonight? Have you gone back to our place at rue Vielle du Temple—the one with the red front?

He's referring to this unassuming steak house in the Marais where we had one of the best crème brûlées in Paris. We must have eaten there at least five times during our stay.

Valentina: No, I'd rather not. Too many memories.

William: Val ...

I worry my lower lip, staring at the screen. I want to shatter it.

Valentina: Anyway, I've got to let you go. A neighbor invited me over for dinner, and I haven't showered yet.

William: A neighbor? Is this neighbor a man?

MIA ASHER

I lower my defenses and allow myself to think of Sébastien for the first time since I left him standing outside my apartment last night. *Is this how it was for William when he first met her? Did he take one glance at her and his day didn't suck so much after all?*

Valentina: No. The couple from downstairs are having a dinner party. I met her on the elevator earlier today, and she asked me to join them. What about you?

William: Going out for a drink with Larry. When are you coming home?

Valentina: I don't know …

It's like he's standing on one side and I'm on the other and there's this space between us that keeps growing and growing, leaving a huge, gaping hole in what used to be our marriage. A minute passes by without an answer. Feeling deflated, I put the phone away. What did I expect? That he would beg me to come home because he needs me?

After the shower, I put on a simple, elegant black dress and classic pointy black pumps. My long hair is up in a ballerina bun. I step away from the full-length mirror to inspect myself. Shrugging, I reach for the clutch lying on the peach accent chair next to me. This is as good as it's going to get.

I briefly consider calling Joanna to excuse myself from dinner, but then I remember my texts with William. It takes every ounce of will I own to finish getting ready when all I want to do is stay in bed, binge eat ice cream, and feel sorry for myself. However, the last thing I need tonight is to be alone while playing the heroine of a melodrama. Conversation and wine, lots of it actually, will help to take my mind off of the whole thing, anesthetizing the pain, even if it's only for a couple of hours.

The dinner party turns out to be more than the small gathering I expected. There are at least eight other couples when I get there. I hand a bottle of wine to the waiter who opens the door and then go in search of the hosts Joanna and Jacob. The soundtrack of jazz music, the clink of crystal glasses, conversation in different languages, and laughter play in the background. I'm calm and relaxed, almost detached, as I glance around the stylish apartment.

Memories of hosting and attending these kinds of parties almost every weekend with William by my side intrude. All eyes were on my husband who could work a room with his charm, charisma, and ease like no other. Women and men of all ages, seasoned players, new and old money, politicians, Hollywood stars. You name it. No one stood a chance against William when he made you the object of his attention. Once, a senator from Florida had told William that The White House could be his future if he chose. And I, his faithful wife, would stand next to him proudly sharing him with others. Watching them lose their minds over him as I understood, maybe too well, what it felt like.

But I lock those memories away before they have a chance to cause any real harm. *Not tonight,* I repeat inside my head. *Tonight the past remains where it belongs—in the past.*

"*Excusez moi.*" I smile tentatively at a couple who moves to the side to let me through.

I'm about to reach for a glass of wine from a passing waiter when I hear Joanna's posh British accent calling my name. I turn to face her, smiling. Lovely and graceful Joanna who looks as though she belongs in the pages of a book with dukes and countesses. She doesn't walk. She glides in her designer shoes.

"Valentina! There you are. I was beginning to despair." She kisses the air on both of my cheeks. "You look ravishing."

I laugh. "So do you. Thank you for having me, Joanna. Your home is lovely."

"It is, isn't it?" She links her arm with mine. "Come, let me introduce you to my husband and to the rest of the guests." She smiles slyly. "There's someone who's been asking about you, actually."

"Really?" I frown. "Who?" *I don't know anyone in Paris. Well, except ...* my heart begins to race.

"Yes, really." She laughs airily, patting my hand. "Can you not take a guess? Maybe I should keep it a surprise?"

We join a group of people standing near a grand piano, dropping the subject. She introduces me to her husband Jacob and to a very famous photographer named Ronan who I recognize from an art magazine and his drop-dead gorgeous fiancée Blaire. They are from New York, too.

After chatting about Paris and New York and the merits of each city, I politely excuse myself and go in search of a drink. As I'm approaching the home bar, a prickle of awareness makes me spin around. I expect to find someone watching me, but everyone seems to be lost in conversation. I rub the back of my neck, dismissing the feeling.

I'm reaching for a glass of wine from the counter when someone comes up behind me. "Hello, ma petite chouette." His breath fans my back as he leans in to grab a drink, making my skin prickle in excitement.

Sébastien. I should be surprised, but I'm not. Deep down, I knew it was him as soon as Joanna mentioned someone asking about me. Or, if I'm honest with myself, I *hoped* it would be him.

The corners of my mouth tilt up on their own volition, feeling like a thirteen-year-old tasting for the first time the delicious, heady flavor of infatuation. "Hi."

This close to him, I can see how thick and curly his eyelashes are. The scruff covering his jaw. And those lips that invite you to fantasize about them in the dirtiest, most forbidden ways. Which I have. "What are you doing here?"

He raises an eyebrow, a faint smile spreading across his handsome face. "Isn't it obvious?"

Charmed by the man standing in front of me, his words fill me with unwanted pleasure. I recline my back on the counter and take a sip of the spicy blend, pretending I didn't hear what he said. Funny how just his presence alone can breathe life into what was a dull party. Suddenly the wine is *sweeter*. The colors more *vibrant*. The room *warmer*.

I focus on Joanna and her husband. They laugh freely and work the room like the born entertainers they are. "It's because of you then."

He leans back, setting his elbows on the counter. His movements easy and graceful remind me of a predator about to strike his unsuspecting prey. "What's that?"

"Why I was invited tonight."

He gives me a sly and sideways grin. "Would it make a difference?"

"I don't know." My lips quirk behind the glass before I take a sip. "Maybe."

"Good maybe or bad maybe?"

"Would it make a difference?" I shoot him a side-glance, throwing back his own words.

He laughs, amusement shining in his eyes. *"Bien, ma petite chouette. Très bien."*

"Merci." A runaway smile escapes my lips. Out of the corner of my eye, I notice that he's wearing a tailored white dress shirt with three buttons carelessly undone at the neck, its sleeves rolled up showcasing his gorgeous arms, and navy blue trousers. His raven locks fall loosely down over his forehead, lending him an air of recklessness and caged energy. He should look untidy in a room where every man is dressed to the nines, but somehow he manages to outshine them all. What chance does a fine suit jacket have against arms like his? None.

Seconds pass in charged silence. This would be the perfect time to go, but I remain in my spot. I don't understand why I linger in his company. I have more common sense than to be attracted to a man who happens to smile and make one feel like her insides are Jell-O.

He says something. I look up as he's smiling down at me, and I realize that, yes, maybe I have no common sense left at all. I clear my throat. "What did you say?"

"I said I'm glad you came, Valentina."

I hear a man's loud laughter coming from somewhere in the room as I get lost in the captivating blue of Sébastien's eyes. If it's a warning, I ignore it. A wiser person would take their leave now, maybe making an excuse about mingling with others. Recognizing the danger in front of her. But sometimes all the reasoning in the world is useless against a lethal man who looks at you as though you're the only woman in the room—who makes you come alive. "Me too."

"Tell me, Valentina, do you believe in fate?"

"Hmm … I don't know. Maybe, yes. I think we can affect our own fates, but I also believe there's this powerful thing—energy, some might call it God—that gives us a nudge in the right direction. How about you?"

"Yeah." His gaze burns into mine, melting me into a puddle. "I think I'm beginning to."

At that moment, another guest walks up to the bar to order a drink. Smiling at him, I step to the side to give him room on the counter. Belatedly realizing that I'm now standing dangerously close to Sébastien. I'm about to move when Sébastien's fingers move lightly over my bare arm. The contact of his skin against mine sends enticing electric shocks throughout my body, paralyzing me. Unable to meet his eyes, I try to focus on the people in front of us rather than the intoxicating man standing next to me or the sweet sensation of his fingers. But it's a losing war. He touches me in slow strokes. Up and down. Back and forth. And as much as I fight my attraction to him, I can still feel his heat slowly crawling deep inside, warming me, seducing me.

The music, the people, the laughter, William and our fight from before, it all fades into nothing. The entire world suddenly becomes the small space between us, beating—pulsing—to the rhythm of his touch.

For a brief and very foolish instant, I picture myself reaching for his hand, whispering in his ear to take me back to his apartment. We wouldn't make it past his door before our clothes were discarded on the floor. His mouth on me, on my breasts. His cock inside me. His head thrown back, his beautiful lips whispering *Valentina, Valentina, Valentina*. And just when I didn't think I could debase myself anymore, I would beg him on red knees and a mouth that tasted like him to take me. Beg him to fill the gaping hole that William tore with his hands and his body. Sébastien and I would build a paradise with our sins while I set my whole world on fire and watched it burn to ashes with him moving inside me.

"Valentina! Come here, darling. I'd like to introduce you to someone," Joanna says, breaking the spell of the moment. She focuses on Sébastien and smiles saucily. "Do share her, you rascal. You've kept her long enough, don't you think?"

"No, I don't think so," Sébastien counters smoothly, making her laugh.

Blushing, I take a deep breath and put some much-needed space between Sébastien and me and the images of us guiltily playing in my head. I try to smile at Joanna and nod, feeling as though I'm drunk or disoriented.

"I should go." I look him in the eye, unwilling to admit even to myself that part of me wishes he'd ask me to stay. Because, God help me, I might.

"One day you're going to stop running away from me. And when that day finally comes, I'll be here waiting for you," he whispers softly, his words a caress. "Now go ... before I change my mind and decide it doesn't please me to share you with others after all."

"I'm not yours to share," I say quietly, wondering if he can hear the fast beating of my heart.

"Luckily for me, I'm not one to give up so easily." He tucks a strand of hair behind my ear and slides the side of his finger along my neck ever so gently as he draws his hand back, leaving a trail of desire behind. Time freezes. Every cell in my body sighs in pleasure as it begs for more. "Besides if you keep running into something good, maybe that's fate telling you that you shouldn't let go." He smiles.

He walks away from me. My gaze follows him until he reaches the same woman from the elevator. Noticing him, she smiles with the practiced ease of a woman who knows she's attractive and alluring. He places the same hand with which he touched me not five minutes ago on the small of her back and guides her toward the living room.

I give my head a tiny shake. Get your shit together, Valentina. Falling for a man like Sébastien would not only be stupid and bad for the heart, it would be fatal.

Stepping away from the bar, I go in search of the hosts, putting Sébastien out of my mind. The last thing I need is another complication in my life.

CHAPTER TEN

Sébastien

My feet slip on wet grass. Rain falls hard on my skin, feeling like whiplashes as I run through the forest. I try to catch up to her, ignoring the punishing sounds of thunder, but the distance between us keeps growing. She laughs and tells me to hurry, that we'll be there soon. Hands grasp air. Her name bounces off my tongue over and over again. But she doesn't stop. She never does. My eyes burn. Desperation floods my veins. Her steps take her further away from me until she disappears into the night, and I'm left all alone.

Like always.

Aching for her.

I wake up, drenched in sweat as a current of desperation and sorrow hums underneath my skin. Then I hear the same sound of thunder that haunted me in my sleep cutting through the silence of the room. It raises the small hair on my arms.

Wide awake now, I glance in the direction of the clock.

2:40 a.m.

Fuck.

Sitting up, I rub my eyes with the heels of my hands as the ghosts who I pray to haunt me forever and leave me all at once disperse like fog. I sigh and get out of bed, knowing that I won't be able to fall back asleep. Nothing new there. Insomnia and I, we're old friends.

I'm about to go to my studio to paint when I hear the faint melody of a Spanish guitar coming from outside the French doors. I follow the music that reminds me of a warm summer night in Barcelona. I reach for the handle and open the door that leads to the balcony. Immediately the cool air of the night envelops me like a thick cloak. I go to stand in front of the railing, place my hands on it, and close my eyes. Inhaling deeply, the smell of rain fills my lungs as it wets my fingers.

The Andalusian melody helps to clear my mind, pulling me out of the black hole of my thoughts. I realize the direction of its source. Leaning over the railing, I look directly below me to find Valentina. She's sitting in a metal chair under the protection of my balcony, the same gray cardigan from the other night wrapped around her slim shoulders. My cock stirs at the sight of her, the creamy color of her skin, and that damn gorgeous mouth of hers.

"Hey," I say, the light rain falling down on the back of my head. Like her, the rest of my body is shielded from the rain by the balcony above.

She tilts her neck back, our gazes locking, and smiles softly. "Can't sleep?"

There it is, I think as I watch her—the reprieve from all the darkness around me. Ever since I first saw her across the room, I knew I was fucked. I didn't understand, I still don't, but when my gaze found her, a part of me sighed and said, there she is, what you've been looking for—welcome to the living world once more, old chap. I wanted to taste her like a fine wine, touch her like a sin. And I did. I told myself that I was just trying to help her out of a shitty situation, but I could have simply told Margot that Valentina was with me. She would have been good. Instead, I took her in my arms and kissed her like the starved man I was. I expected a docile partner, a shy kisser, an unwilling accomplice. She was none of those things. She returned my kiss with just as much wanton need as I felt, shaking me to the damn core. As we continued to run into each other, I became addicted to the way she made me feel whenever she was near me. She was like coming up for air after nearly drowning.

"You too?"

She pushes her glasses up by their bridge using a finger. "Yeah, too much going on in my mind. Music keeping you up?" A roguish dimple appears on her left cheek, the dimple that I've wanted to kiss pretty much since the day I noticed it there. "Guess it's my turn, huh? Sorry. I'll turn it down now."

"Music's fine."

"Okay, good." She lifts a hand into the air with her palm facing skyward, collecting raindrops. "It's the first time it's rained since I got here. Paris is lovely when it rains."

I tilt my head back to try to find the moon, aware I should go back inside, but just being close to her soothes me. I find myself relaxing in her company even though it's beginning to rain harder. Bending at the waist, I rest my arms on the railing, focusing on the skyline: The glittering Eiffel Tower in the background, the zigzagged roofs, the empty park across the street, and the few cars driving on the road.

"I got a job," she blurts out.

"You did?" I don't know why, but the fact that she's willing to share this piece of her with me makes me feel invincible, like I've been allowed inside when she doesn't let many people in.

"Yes, it's nothing really. Just helping a man at this flower shop. It should be interesting since he doesn't speak English and I don't speak French." She chuckles. "Thank God for the Internet and dictionaries."

"It's not nothing." A car drives by then, splashing the curb. "Does it make you happy?"

A pause. "Yes. Very much so."

"That's what matters."

"Yes, you're right." She lets out a long sigh. "Joanna and her husband throw a great dinner party. Have you known them long?"

"Ever since I moved here, about six years ago. They're good people."

"I like them. I had a good time tonight." She hesitates, seemingly waging her next words with great care. "What happened to your date?"

So, she was paying attention. I smile, feeling like the motherfucking king of the world, the rain temporarily forgotten. I watch her again. "Jealous?"

"Yeah, right." Valentina crosses her arms over her chest and huffs as though offended by the mere thought. In the dark, I can almost see the sweet blush spreading under her glasses, picture the hitch in her breathing, her perfect tits rising and falling beckoning to me like a siren song. "I'm just surprised that she isn't with you."

I raise an eyebrow. "What makes you think she isn't inside waiting for me?" I tease her.

"Seriously? Of all the—"

"She went home, Valentina. You shouldn't be jealous, you know? She's just a friend. Besides, she's not you."

And it's true. All my relationships after Poppy have been pleasant, full of physical hunger, and attraction. No promises, no strings, just one hell of a good time. I get to numb myself—to escape. She gets a man who will fuck every part of her body, and fuck her good. It might not be much of a life, but it's been enough for me.

That is until Valentina and that kiss …

She's about to say something, probably put me in my place, when my last words seem to register in her pretty head, robbing her of a quick, scathing comeback. A darling confused expression settles on her face. I only wish it was my mouth and not my words that put it there.

Entranced by her, I fail to notice the storm is picking up speed until it's too late. A strong wind blows past us. Another angry roar of thunder strikes. Lightning falls right across from us over by the park, striking the iron bench. "Jesus fucking Christ," I utter. Shaken, I close my eyes while trying to calm the fuck down. And then, they come—the never-failing memories that choke me. What-ifs become punishment rather than escape. Poor pathetic fuck, I think. Even after ten years I'm still affected by this shit. It's like every particle of my body relives that fucking night. What it smelled like when I got out of my car to walk into the hospital. Driving under a night sky illuminated by lightning as thunder boomed in my ears. Rain hitting the windshield. I should remember her laughter or the exact shade of her red hair or the way she felt in my arms, but instead …

I open my eyes, watching drops land on my skin.

Instead I remember this.

After a pause, I hear her voice, soft and sweet, and it calls me back from the hell I'm drowning in. "Sébastien? Are you okay?"

I notice that I'm holding onto the railing with all of my strength while trembling profusely. "I don't know … fuck," I curse, disgusted by the despair in my voice. "I can't right now. I gotta go."

Rudely, I leave without giving her a chance to reply. In the room, I stop after taking no more than a few steps. *What am I doing?* Every part of my being begs to go back outside, already missing and needing her warm light, somehow feeling hollow, empty; but I'm frozen from the inside out. Unable to move. My mind won't stop its torture, just like the rain.

I'm drowning.

I don't know how much time passes until I hear the doorbell ring, making me aware of my surroundings. The next thing I know I'm opening the door and come face to face with Valentina.

"What do you want?" I ask brusquely, holding onto the door. I fight the urge to pull her viciously in my arms and savage her until all the ghosts have left me.

A tiny frown forms on her forehead, her gaze full of concern. "I was worried about you."

"I'm fine," I lie.

"Are you sure? Back there—"

"Yeah. Go back to your apartment." I begin to close the door in her face, but she stops it by placing a small hand on it.

"I don't know. I thought," she tucks a lock of hair behind her ear, "maybe … Would you like some company?"

What I want is to get on my knees and ask you to bless my soulless body, to let me find salvation in yours, but I know it's of no use. "You thought wrong. Now go."

She takes a step forward, seemingly not caring that I want her out of my apartment. "But—"

"Don't come in," I warn her. "Unless you're looking for a fuck."

She flinches at the cruelty of my words, but the soft light in her eyes doesn't disappear. If anything it shines brighter, like a lone star trying to show me the way. She extends a hand to touch me, and I move back as though the contact was poisoning. "Don't."

"You're shaking, Sébastien." Valentina places a palm on my chest, and it's like I'm being branded with a hot iron, her fingers burned into my skin. I want to move, but I don't—I can't. "What's the matter? Please talk to me."

"I don't want to talk." I shake my head. There's a deranged monster inside me who wants blood. The bastard wants to hurt as much as he's hurting. Maybe then the pain will stop.

Cursing, I reach for Valentina and pull her in my arms. "What I want is my cock deep inside you." I dig my fingers into her skin, and run my lips on her shoulder, the elegant line of her neck, filling my mouth to the brim with her taste—to remember or to forget. It's all the same. "Fucking that sweet cunt of yours." My touch turns painful, but Valentina doesn't fight me. I let go of her and cup her perfect tits, sullying her skin with my filthy hands. I want to punish and scare her. And while I'm at it, punish myself too.

"Stop, Sébastien. This isn't like you." She wraps her arms around me, holding on. I try to push her away, but she won't let me go. "Talk to me," she entreats soothingly. "Hey." Her eyes find and hold mine prisoner. "Hey. Come back to me."

Come back. Come back. She pulls me slowly out of the abyss until I'm no longer in the past but here in front of her. And the realization of what I was about to do is a visceral punch to the gut. Head hung low. An earthquake of shame spreads under my skin, leaving destruction behind. I struggle to meet her eyes. "I'm so fucking sorry, ma petite chouette. So damn sorry—"

"Shh … it's okay." She runs a hand over the back of my skull again and again. Slowly the noises fade to a faint echo with each stroke of hers. "It's okay."

"It's the—" I close my eyes. Feel her around me. She brings me comfort like a shot of whiskey. I forget to measure my words and confine my emotions. I let them escape out of me, unfiltered and illogical. And through it all Valentina—this almost stranger who should be running for the hills instead of remaining here—holds me close. "Storms like this … they bring it all back." I envelop her in a tight embrace and bury my face in her neck. Needing to feel her, to know she's real when nothing else seems to be. "Don't leave."

They say time heals all wounds, but I disagree. Grief never ends, it just changes. You learn how to live with it, rebuild yourself from the shattered pieces around you until you're whole again, but you will never be the same. The light is gone. The flavors. The laughter. You become a stranger who you used to know. But then one day you wake up, and you find the dark has been penetrated by a spark in the shape of a slip of woman with brown eyes that could drive a man to perdition.

"I won't."

I shudder in relief. My mind shuts down. *She's here*, I tell myself. And for now that's more than enough. It's everything.

CHAPTER ELEVEN

Sébastien

I BLINK A COUPLE of times and notice that it's morning already, the sunlight filtering through the curtains, warm on my face. I reach for my phone on the nightstand, blindly grabbing item after item until locating it, and look at the time. My eyes widen in surprise. *No shit.* Well, this is a first. 10:40 a.m. I slept. A smile tugs the corners of my mouth. And like a damn baby, too. I'm rested—relaxed. There's a new, strange feeling, though. One I had forgotten all about, and that is of being at peace.

Then I remember.

Valentina. Her softness. I wanted to hold her close to me for as long as I could. Cling to her sweet words. Sink my claws into her as she told me everything would be all right.

She took me to my bedroom, helped me out of my soaked shirt, and went in search of a new one for me to wear. There were no more words spoken. Silence and her presence were all I needed, and she knew it. Her fingers grazed my skin as she helped me into a clean tee, her touch tender, giving—asking for nothing in return. I wanted to weep at her feet.

Suddenly bone tired, I fell flat on my stomach on the bed. For a moment, I was afraid that she would leave, but I should have known better. This was Valentina, and she was brave and kind.

She sat next to me with her back reclined against the wall, her bare thigh so close to my lips it would have been easy to reach for her and bury my face between her legs. And by God, I wanted to. But I didn't. Closing my eyes, I took a deep breath, filling my lungs with the smell of woman and Valentina. It would have to do. She reached for my hand then, holding the shattered pieces of me without being afraid to be cut by them, and sleep finally came.

Sitting up on the bed, I scratch the back of my neck and glance around the room. The door to the bathroom is closed, and my clothes from last night lay in a neat pile on the brown leather seat by the door—Valentina's doing, I'm sure. Everything appears as it should.

Did she leave?

The thought fills me with disappointment. *Man, you've got it bad.* Shaking my head, I chuckle sheepishly, push the sheets to the side, and get out of bed. I'm stretching when the smell of coffee drifts into the room. I open the door and stop as my eyes greedily take in the scene unfolding in my kitchen. Frozen. Mouth on the floor. Feeling like a kid in a candy shop.

Completely unaware of me, I watch Valentina slow dance as she cooks something on the stove while humming a familiar tune, but the food is the last thing on my mind. I grin like a son of a bitch, reclining on the doorframe, cross my arms, and enjoy the show. *Thank you, baby Jesus. I owe you one, man.* My eyes are glued to her slim hips swaying from side to side, pleasure and decadence in her every move. Her whole body curves and bends to the rhythm of the music in her head, and I see no traces of the stuck-up, standoffish woman from the gallery. No, this woman is wild, untamed, passionate, and so damn sexy—the one I see glimpses of once in a while in the way she laughs, the way she stares at me when she thinks I'm not paying attention, and, goddamn, in the way she kisses.

Snap out of it, loser, I tell myself. But then the cardigan slips down her arm to reveal the soft skin of her shoulder. An unbidden image of her straddling my lap flashes before my eyes. She would roll her hips on my cock, my fingers digging in the soft skin of her ass while my tongue finds that same spot on her shoulder where I would discover what sin tastes like.

Nope. No can do. I'm fucked. Royally fucked.

71

And just when I think Valentina can't surprise me anymore, she lifts the spatula in her hand and uses it as a pretend-microphone. Losing herself in the song, she sings about trying to hold back a feeling for so long. She asks if you feel like she does. Throwing her heart into the chorus, she misses the notes of the come ons and oohs, but no one watching her would give a damn. They'd be goners like me. She sings endearingly out of tune, and I go from wanting to fuck her brains out to wanting to kiss her silly until her lips only know mine.

She twirls once for the grand finale and shrieks when she finds me there. "Oh my God." A hand to the chest, shock and embarrassment register in her lovely features. "I thought you were still sleeping. How long have you been standing there?"

I push myself away from the doorframe, strolling toward her, enjoying the blush spreading through her cheeks. The inner savage, hunter, caveman in me shouts, *Mine. Mine. Mine. All mine.* "Not long enough."

Valentina places the spatula on a white plate next to the stove in a very ladylike manner and turns off the burner. Gone is the careless girl from a moment ago, and I want her back. "I hope you enjoyed the show."

Five steps separate us.

"You've got no idea."

Four steps ...

Flustered, she straightens her cardigan, crosses her arms over her chest, and leans her back against the counter.

Three steps ...

"What song was that anyway?"

Two ...

She strokes the back of her neck, trying not to fidget under my appreciative gaze. "You know ... 'Let's Get It On'?"

I'm now standing so close to her, we might as well be touching. Towering over her, I grin wickedly as I place my hands on the counter, enclosing her within my arms. "Yes. Let's," I whisper softly.

She blinks repeatedly as though disoriented. "I-I meant the song by Marvin Gaye."

"That was Marvin Gaye?"

"I was a little off."

I raise an eyebrow, the corners of my mouth twitch. "Is that so?"

LOVE ME IN THE DARK

"Okay, maybe a lot off." She laughs openly, her eyes a swirl of chocolate and caramel behind the glasses.

Ah. There she is again.

"Are you hungry? I made breakfast."

"Depends. Are you as good of a cook as you are a singer?" I tease her, enjoying myself more than I should, more than it's safe. "Because if you are ..." I pretend to grimace.

She smacks my chest playfully. "Jerk."

We laugh, and it feels as good as a smoke after an energetic fuck. Silence falls when laughter disappears and all that is left are lingering smiles on our lips. I could get used to this—her presence filling the empty rooms in my home—laughing. The unbidden thought takes me by surprise. But once planted, it grows like a seed, its roots taking hold of me.

I stare, my eyes devouring her as I try to memorize the exact location of the tiny beauty mark close to her lips. *Top left, right by her dimple—my own Bermuda Triangle.* "Thank you for last night," I say huskily.

"Don't worry about it. I did what anyone in my position would've done." She looks nervously around, avoiding my gaze. "Besides, you have a lovely guest room with a very comfortable bed. You know ... I-I think it's time for me to go. Enjoy breakfast." She tries to escape like a hunted animal, nudging my arm to move.

But I don't let her. I tighten my grip on the edges of the counter. "Why did you stay?"

"Because you asked me to."

"You could've left after I fell asleep." My heart kicks into overdrive. Time seems to freeze as she considers her next words carefully.

"Because I wanted to stay," she whispers. "And it felt nice ..."

I lean closer to her. My lips brush her earlobe. "What did?"

"Being needed." She raises her gaze, meeting mine.

And what I see is like a punch to the gut. I want to fly to New York and kill that motherfucker husband of hers, beat him down to a pulp with my own hands for having dared to put that pain in her eyes.

"Wanted. I-I had forgotten what it felt like and ... and—"

"You've got no idea, do you?" I brush the hair away from her shoulder with the back of my fingers. She trembles under me. Trace the elegant line of her neck and shoulder with hands that desire to conquer and dominate—that long to own her.

She releases a shaky breath. "What's that?"

"*J'ai envie de toi.*" I take her wrist in my hand and kiss the inside, feeling the pulse as it beats life back into mine. "*J'ai besoin de toi. Tu me rends fou.*" Wish my lips could embed the words on her skin, show and make her believe them. I let go of the wrist to cup her face, my thumb stroking the inebriating blush on her cheek. "If I were a weaker man—"

Valentina licks her lips, her chest rising and falling brokenly. "Yes?"

The incessant ring of the doorbell breaks the moment as though cold water has been poured down on us. I let her go, cursing under my breath. Valentina staggers back as I realize how close I came to losing control of the situation. Jesus Christ. One more minute and I would have ravaged her on the kitchen counter.

"You should really lock your door, you know, Sébastien," a familiar voice says teasingly from somewhere behind us. "We were in the neighborhood and thought we should surprise you—Oh. Looks like—uh—hello!"

This can't be happening. But Valentina's mortified expression tells me it is. Trying to cover herself, she pulls the cardigan closer about her.

"Uncle Sebs! Uncle Sebs!" A little urchin with black curls comes running toward me, wrapping his little arms around my legs. "Lowk!" He tilts his head back, giving me a shit-eating grin. "I lost a tooth!"

"Awesome, buddy. Why don't you tell me all about it later?" I ruffle little Jack's curls while looking at my cousin Sophie, her husband, and niece.

Ever since Jack, Sophie's husband, became the new Ambassador of the United States to France, and they moved here all the way from D.C., they've tried to adopt me as the fifth member of their family. They are gawking at Valentina and me with eyes as wide as saucers, bags in their arms filled with food worthy of feeding an army. I would laugh if it weren't for Valentina and how this affects her.

An innate desire to protect Valentina from embarrassment prompts me to stand next to her. "Well, this is definitely a surprise. I wasn't expecting you guys." I throw a quick glance at Valentina, the kind that says I'm sorry and understand if I'm in the doghouse, before introducing her to my family.

After the initial shock, Valentina seems to relax. The introductions are made. Everyone laughs the whole thing off as a good joke. And if she's aware what this must appear to my family, she takes it in stride. The only telltale sign of any lingering embarrassment is the soft blush on her cheeks.

"Who are you?" Needing his own introduction, little Jack asks Valentina with the openness of a child barely five years old. I'm about to tell him to mind his own business when she surprises me once again.

She focuses on my nephew as a soft expression crosses her face that makes me think she's the most beautiful thing I've ever seen. My fingers itch to paint her, capture her just as she is right now. Without an ounce of pride or reserve, just the real Valentina.

"Come here, Jack," his father orders. "Leave the lady alone."

"It's okay." She smiles at my family members and then focuses all of her attention on little Jack who's eyeing her with curiosity. "I'm Valentina and I'm your Uncle Sebs's friend. How do you do?"

"Good. I lost a tooth, and I didn't cry when Daddy pull it out. There was blood *everywhere*." He grins, showing her the gap. "See. Do you know the Tooth Fairy? She left me five Euros."

"What a brave boy you are."

"Yep." He turns to Sophie who's watching him with a motherly pride. "Mommy, per'aps you can invite her for dinner at our house instead of the other ladies that Uncle Sebs didn't like."

The matchmaking wheels set in motion, Sophie claps in excitement. "But what a splendid idea!"

Jack snorts. "You're in trouble, man." He looks at Valentina and mouths the word "run," which makes her laugh.

"*Really* ... How many have there been?" Valentina asks laughingly, joining the let's-roast-Uncle-Sebs-party.

"Tons." He scrunches up his nose in dislike. "And one pinched my cheek very hard. I didn't like it."

Isabella, the little minx, joins in. "Oh, and the lady with the red shoes who hated men."

I shrug. "Yeah, that one was doomed from the beginning."

Everyone bursts out laughing, and the kitchen once devoid of life is now bursting with it. My eyes find Valentina, like they always do. My family members fade into the meaningless background as we stare at each other.

She smiles at me.

And there it is again ...

The light.

Hope.

CHAPTER
TWELVE
Valentina

In a haze, I make it back to my place after staying for breakfast at Sébastien's. I go to the bathroom, turn the shower on. The clothes kiss my skin as they fall to the marble floor, and I jump in. I tilt my head back and close my eyes. The hot water covers me from head to toe, the steam rising around me.

My movements are methodical, but my mind is somewhere else, bursting with memories. The night and morning tangle together like a never-ending loop. Going to his apartment after he fled the balcony. Seeing the grief, the desolation, the utter hopelessness in his eyes as he opened the door. He wanted to push me away, but I wasn't going to let him. I didn't know what to do, but the necessity to shield him from his own pain, to be there for him in his moment of need, became vital to me. Therefore I offered myself to his ravaging agony. I thought, *take this body. Punch it with your words. Scar it with your hands. But come back to me. Bring back the Sébastien I've come to know.*

The anger vibrating in his arms as I held him should have scared me. However, my only thoughts were that he was hurting, that he needed me. A flood of questions inundated my mind, but I knew he wasn't ready to share answers with me just yet, so I just held him through it all.

When sleep came for him at last, I thought about leaving but I took one glance at his hand entwined with mine, and I knew I couldn't. Just like I know something changed in our relationship. A nameless moment that filled the never-ending quiet—the kind of small moment life is made out of.

I reach for the shampoo, pour some into my hand, enjoying its fruity smell of berries, before massaging it into my scalp. I smile as I think of this morning.

The laughter ... the banter ... the companionship ... his lips on my skin ... what I saw in his eyes, a direct reflection of mine, right before we were interrupted ... his lovely family as they tried to make me feel welcome.

It should have been too much. Too overwhelming. Red flags should have been waved. Sirens heard. But all I could think was that I couldn't remember the last time I'd felt this happy or when I'd had such a good time.

Sébastien's parting words as we stood outside his apartment intrude my mind like a midnight robber, sobering me up.

"There's a party tomorrow night at Plaza Athénée. I'd like you to come with me."

"I don't think I should."

"Why not?"

"I don't know how to do this, Sébastien." I point a finger between the two of us, thinking of a million reasons why I shouldn't even contemplate the idea of going. "When you're around ..." I find myself wanting you more and more. I bite my lower lip. "I'm afraid I'll come to regret all of this."

He chuckles. "You know, regrets aren't such a bad thing. Sometimes giving fear the middle finger can feel fucking good." He taps my nose gently. "I'll be at the party until eleven."

"What happens if I don't go?"

"But, ma petite chouette, what if you do?"

It's just an invitation.

But, somehow, it seems more than that.

CHAPTER THIRTEEN

IT'S SO EASY TO blame others for one's mistakes. That way we don't have to be held accountable for whatever part, big or small, we've played. I could place the blame on William's shoulders as to why I'm here, standing outside the famous hotel. I could blame his disloyalty for each step I make that brings me closer to a man who isn't him—my husband.

But deep down, I will always know I'm here because I want to be.

All day yesterday and today, I tried to come up with empty excuses that would stop me from coming. *It will give Sébastien the wrong idea. It will be very unwise and foolish of me. I want him, and I shouldn't. Nothing good will come from it.* However, none of those excuses stopped me from checking the time, from counting down the hours.

And as I got ready, choosing a form-fitting muted silver dress with spaghetti straps and a plunging back, I deliberately thought about everything with the exception of whom I was dressing for and where I was going. *Seems like I've gotten really good at lying to myself.*

I am now standing at the entrance of the hall searching for him, and that's when I can't continue pretending anymore. Truth of the matter is that I never had any intention of not coming.

Dry throat. Sweaty palms. Excitement runs rampant through my veins with each step I take. The room pulses with life and music and the buzz of conversation. The smell of flowers coats the air like a cocoon. Expensive champagne and wine fuel the licentious behavior of people around me. It's all the more thrilling because I know he's here and because I shouldn't be.

I spot him standing by the bar surrounded by a group of people. Mesmerized, I pause to take him in. Sébastien. A thief amongst kings. And how he shines against a backdrop that is already blinding in its splendor. He's laughing at something when his eyes connect with mine. Instantly, the room disappears, dissolving to dust, except for the two of us. He smiles a smile that could melt gold, one that I know is only for me. He slowly raises the flute in a silent toast before bringing it to his lips and taking a sip as he watches me over the rim of the glass. My ears begin to buzz. I lick my lips almost expecting to taste the champagne on mine—to taste him.

My feet begin to move of their own accord. As the space between us disappears, so does my guilt. Tomorrow when I'm no longer under his spell, when the truth is staring at me right in the face and I can't deny it anymore, I'll deal with the consequences.

But not tonight.

Without taking his eyes off of me, Sébastien excuses himself from the group as he signals me with a barely perceptible nod of his head to follow him. He walks toward an empty balcony to the left of the bar, far away from all the hubbub and the guests. While I silently trail after him, I observe both women and men hungrily watching his every step while moving to the side to let him through.

He reaches the balcony first. With less than five steps separating us, I pause to take a deep breath while gathering my courage, and step out into the night. Sébastien glances back, and our eyes lock until I come to stand next to him.

"I feel like I should say, 'Surprise, I came!' or something like that, but you always knew I'd come, didn't you?" Sébastien turns his body toward mine, leans down and places a kiss on each of my cheeks. He's deliberately slow, taking his time as his lips make contact with my skin, setting a massive amount of butterflies loose in my stomach. And they turn from butterflies to lions roaring inside me. "I didn't, but I hoped you would."

Dizzy, I place my hands on the iron railing for support. Suddenly unable to meet his gaze, I focus on the Eiffel Tower shining brightly and illuminating the night sky as its beam lights up the city. I try to make sense of the inner turmoil this maddening man causes inside me, but it's of no use. There's no logic to it. No reason. How can I put down into words what he awakens in me with his mere proximity when I can barely understand it?

"I love the way the Eiffel Tower sparkles."

"They are golden lights that go on every night, every hour on the hour."

"It's beautiful. Makes me think that it's covered in stars. Great party, by the way."

"It is now."

Blushing, I pretend I didn't hear him even though my legs suddenly don't feel strong enough. A smile crosses my lips as I trace the railing with my fingertip, secretly loving his words. How can Sébastien be so absurd and yet so endearing at the same time?

He bumps my shoulder with his. "Did I say something amusing?"

I shake my head, thinking that now would be the perfect time to change the subject. "How was your day?"

Out of the corner of my eye, I see him smile as though he knows what I just did and why. "Really, Valentina? You're asking me about my day? Next, you'll talk about the weather."

I laugh. "Seemed the polite thing to do."

A couple steps outside onto the balcony next to ours. She has blond hair and long red nails. I frown. Something about her seems familiar. The man and woman don't waste any time, losing themselves in their embrace.

"So ... Paris. How's it treating you?" I hear Sébastien ask, drawing back my attention to him.

"Who's being polite now?"

"Trying to behave here."

"Really?" I arch an eyebrow, teasing him. "*You? Behave?* Do you ever?"

"Sometimes."

"Like you're doing right now?"

Spellbound, I watch Sébastien raise a hand to caress the arc of my cheek with the back of his fingers as a strand of hair falls across his forehead. His lips curve sinfully. His heavy-lidded eyes fall upon my mouth. "Oui, ma petite chouette, even though good behavior is the last thing on my mind at the moment."

I laugh as his words send a current of excitement and shivers shooting right through me, coating my body in heat. *I want him. I want him inside of me. I want to know the taste of his seed on my tongue. The force of his thrusts. And most of all, I want this. The laughter. The butterflies. Him.* I stare at the skyline and its timeless architecture, taking a deep breath, trying to smother the hunger of my body and my heart. I clear my throat. "So. Paris. I was walking around the city the other day. Rediscovering it, really."

"Funny that. I'd assumed this was your first time."

"No." I shake my head, meeting his gaze again. "My first on my own, though."

"I see." A shadow crosses over his face, darkening his eyes and dimming their light fleetingly. But he blinks, and it's gone. "And has it changed since?"

"Not really. But the way I view it has. Ever watch *Runaway Bride?*"

"Can't say that I have." He pulls a packet of cigarettes out of the inside pocket of his tuxedo, offers me one, but I politely decline. After a short nod, he lights one, takes a drag, blowing out the smoke through his mouth and nose. "Any good?"

As the smoke curls like a snake in the air, I'm tempted to ask him for a drag, just so I can place my lips where his have been ...

Focus. Movie. Right.

"Well, I think so, but then again, romantic movies are right in my wheelhouse." I throw him a conspiratorial glance, grinning. "Especially the cheesy holiday ones."

He grins back. "Really?"

"Oh, yeah. Hallmark sucker, here. Anyway ... Julia. Runaway Bride. There's this scene in the movie where Richard Gere asks Julia's character what kind of eggs she likes. I can't remember exactly what she said, but it was something along the lines of, 'Whatever you like or whatever you're having.' You see, she didn't know how she liked her eggs because she always ate them the same way the man she happened to be with at the time preferred them."

Cigarette back to his lips. Inhales. Exhales. "Sounds like she didn't know her mind."

"Exactly. So then, Gere's character asks her, 'No, what kind of eggs do *you* like?'" I pause, worrying my lip. God, I'd really kill for that cigarette now. "I've done a lot of thinking since I got here. Soul-searching, I guess. And like Julia's character, I've realized *I* don't know how I like my eggs either. Somehow, somewhere along the line, I forgot who I am, what I like and what I don't. I've been so focused on pleasing my husband, fitting in his world, that I forgot about *me*.

"Don't get me wrong. It's not his fault. He never forced me to change. I did it all because I wanted to."

My aunt once told me that women marry men hoping that they can change them, but they can't. And men marry women hoping they'll never change, but they always do. But when I met William, I didn't see a man who I wanted to change to fit *me*. I didn't want to tame him. He was perfect the way he was. Instead, I wanted to change so I could be worthy of *him*.

Shaking my head, I smile sadly. "I'm sorry ... I'm unloading all of my emotional BS with you, and it's probably the last thing you want to hear. The baggage of a bored, messed-up housewife."

"Don't be so hard on yourself. We're all fucked up in our own little ways. Besides, love can be like that. Make one fly so damn high, you're blind to the fall. And, sometimes, even if you see it—know that there's no way you'll survive it—you just don't give a damn because it feels damn fucking good."

I clear my throat, looking away, and stare down at the street. I focus on a black car driving away—it's less risky for my peace of mind and heart. Just when I think the storm has passed and I've made it out alive, he reaches for my hand tentatively, softly, and the touch is more intimate than a kiss could ever be, more devastating. Every atom in my body attuned to him, begging him silently to never let me go, to stay right here with me just holding my hand. He turns it over, so my palm is facing up, and he covers it with his. No words are spoken. There's no need for them. The silence is comfortable like the warm breeze kissing my skin.

"Where do you go from here?"

"What do you mean?"

"One must live. Fall. Fail. Get up. Try again and again until we get it right. Life is too short to not know how you like your eggs, Valentina."

"I don't know." I pause, watching people walk by, trying to guess their destinations, thinking of Guillaume and the flower shop and how good it felt to get the job, to have a purpose. "Maybe ... Maybe find out if I like to dance in the rain. What it feels like to stay up all night and watch the sunrise. Pretend to be someone else for a day for kicks and giggles."

"Look at me, Valentina," he orders gently.

Hesitantly, always hesitantly when it comes to him, I will myself to meet his eyes.

"You're more than what you give yourself credit for."

"I don't know about that," I scoff, trying to hide my glass-thin vulnerability behind a beat-up armor.

"You know what I see when I look at you?"

I give my head a tiny shake.

"When I look at you I see a woman who might've lost her way, but I *know* she's brave enough to find it back. She knows it too. She just needs a little push in the right direction."

Silence grows and matures like a tree around us. He raises his hand, as though in slow motion or a dream, sliding it under my hair. He molds his palm along the nape of my neck, his thumb stroking my hot skin, replacing the blood in my veins with liquid lava.

"What are you thinking about?" I whisper.

Sébastien leans forward until our faces are dangerously close. My mind shouts at me to move, but I unwisely ignore it while drowning in an ocean of blue. Every part of my body tingles.

"That I've never wanted to kiss someone like I want to kiss you right now."

A pause that tastes bitter like betrayal.

"I'm married."

Another pause. This one tastes like regret, hopelessness.

He rubs his thumb over my jawline, my bottom lip. "Why did you come then, Valentina?"

"Because I wanted to. Because I need to be where you are. Because when I'm with you, I'm happy."

Somewhere deep in the recesses of my mind, I register the sound of people laughing, the honking of a car, the siren of an ambulance—life moving around us as though nothing is out of the ordinary. It all fades to a meaningless nothing because of a man who holds me as though I'm the most precious thing he's ever held.

Breathing hard, I grab him by the wrist. His skin is smooth and hard, warm and inviting. And I never want to let go even though I should.

"Say something," I whisper.

"Your husband is a fool. If you were mine ..." He takes me by surprise when he lowers his face and kisses each of my fingers. His demanding lips send shockwaves running through me. "Jesus Christ, Valentina, you make me feel things I never thought would be possible to feel again," he croaks, kissing my forehead. The laughing man has been replaced by a somber stranger, one whose eyes are full of pain and desperation. I want to pull him into my arms and hold onto him through the pain once again. "I look at you and I dare to hope even though—"

"Valentina? Is that you?" I hear a familiar voice ask, breaking the spell of the moment.

No. No. No! I curse the gods who keep interrupting us as I guiltily step away from Sébastien and put some space between us, turning in the direction of the woman's voice.

"Gigi?" Shock slices through me as I watch my friend step into the light. Soul Cycled legs. Cherry red lips. She's wearing a mini red dress that leaves very little to the imagination. Georgiana "Gigi" Stanhope. A sex bomb. A fixture in social magazines and fundraisers. And who happens to be married to one of William's best friends and partners. "What are you doing here?"

"Looks like the same thing as you." She grins as she checks out Sébastien unashamedly. "Enjoying myself, Val."

A guilty blush burns my cheeks. "I didn't know you were coming to Paris. I mean, last time we spoke, you said you had nothing planned."

"That time at Neiman's, right?" She shrugs, and even her shrug is seductive. "Change of plans." She reaches for a blond god, who appears to be much younger than us, and snakes her hands around his tuxedo-clad arm. "I decided to treat myself instead. Val, meet Ryan. Ryan, meet Valentina."

I introduce them to Sébastien, and we shoot the breeze for a little. There aren't any uncomfortable silences because of Gigi's continuous chatter. A natural born entertainer, all eyes and attention must be on her at all times. I don't mind it. I actually prefer it that way. It gives me time to think of an answer in case she asks me about William or Sébastien. Or of an excuse to leave without being rude.

She reaches for my hand. "Val, come with me. Gentlemen, we'll be back in a few. Don't do anything that I wouldn't do."

"Which is not much," I say sarcastically under my breath, making her laugh.

She guides me to a ladies' bathroom, opening all the doors of the stalls to make sure we're alone. When she's satisfied, she moves toward the marble counter, reclines her hip against it, and crosses her arms. "Now, answer two things, you naughty girl. Where is that hapless husband of yours? And, most importantly, how in the world did you end up in the arms of Sébastien Leroux? Not that I blame you one bit."

"You know him?"

"We went to the same boarding school in Switzerland for a while, but I don't think he recognizes me." She shakes her head. "Gods like him didn't mingle with mere humans. He was a few years ahead of me, but whispers of what he could do to a woman's body followed him everywhere. And he was just a kid then. Thinking of how he is now ..." She pretends to fan herself, leaning forward as though she were going to tell me a secret. "Have you fucked him yet?"

"There's nothing between us," I'm quick to add, blushing and beyond uncomfortable.

"Okay," she replies, a sly grin on her face. "If you say so. He's quite the catch, you know? World-renowned artist, sex god extraordinaire, and independently wealthy. Dad was some kind of Wall Street King. Mom was a famous French actress. So I ask you again, how did you end up in his arms, you *lucky, lucky* girl?"

"I wasn't in his arms."

"Oh, babe. You're so full of shit your eyes are brown."

I stand next to her, reclining my hips against the marble counter, and bump her shoulder with mine. "You know, for an egomaniac, you notice too much."

She has the decency to laugh.

"William is back home. And I'm here, trying to figure out my next step," I say, suddenly feeling deflated. Being next to her brings it all back, injecting a dose of stark reality into the fantasy world I've been living in for the past few days.

Understanding shines in Gigi's eyes. "I was really mad for you when Larry told me what happened. Like seriously? Fucking the intern? Couldn't he have been less cliché?" She nods towards the door of the bathroom. "Ryan, out there. He's my divorce gift to myself."

My eyes widen. "Wait, what? I didn't know you and Larry were having problems."

"Yep. The asshole traded me for a newer model, so I upgraded too."

I place a hand on her diamond-covered wrist. "I'm sorry, Gigi."

She pats my hand. "Oh, don't be sorry for me. Be sorry for Larry. My lawyers are better than his."

We chat a little bit more about the proceedings of her divorce. If she notices I'm avoiding the subject of my own marriage, she doesn't mention it. Besides, what is there to say? That it's pretty much over?

We leave the bathroom and join the guys who are waiting for us in the same place. As soon as I spot Sébastien, I feel like the air is back in my lungs, and when his smiling eyes meet mine, I can breathe again. If this is wrong, I can't bring myself to care.

Sébastien places his hand on the small of my back, touching bare skin. Possessively. Unashamedly. He claims that part of my body and my body surrenders with a shivering sigh. Leaning close to my ear, he whispers enticing words, "Want to get out of here?"

And an even more dangerous answer forms in my chest, in the back of my throat, on my tongue, in the tip of my fingers. *God, yes.*

"Yes."

CHAPTER FOURTEEN

HE TAKES MY HAND as I pick up the front of my dress and follow him. Laughter bubbles inside me, out of me. At this moment, we are young, reckless, eternal, and alive. So fucking alive. Hair-raising electricity courses through me. He steals a champagne bottle from a passing waiter. We're not walking anymore. We're running past strangers, past crowds of angry people. It doesn't matter. It all becomes a blur around me except for the solid warmth in my hand guiding me away from the darkness and towards safety like a beacon full of light.

We make it outside. Chests heaving. Street lamps bathing our surroundings in an amber haze. A tornado of happiness and exhilaration threaten to sweep me away.

I look up at the night sky full of stars shining like little diamonds. Spread my arms and twirl one or two times, feeling free. "Beautiful, aren't they? The stars?"

"Yes, very beautiful."

Glancing in his direction, I find him watching me closely instead. Pleasure settles deep in my core, making my entire body throb with yearning.

Sébastien brings the green bottle to his lips and chugs down some of the champagne, drinking it with gusto and pleasure. When he's finished, he hands it to me with a secret smile in his eyes. I stare at the bottle for a second and think *what-the-hell.*

Sebastien says, amusement carried in his tone.

Sorry. That felt good," I say, smiling shyly. "Tasted good, too."

Throwing caution and manners to the wind, I let go and reach for the champagne. And I drink, and drink, and drink. I drink as though all my life I'd been dying of thirst and this is the first time my mouth has tasted water.

"Easy there," Sébastien says, amusement carried in his tone.

Laughing and choking a little at the same time, I hand the bottle back to him as I wipe my mouth with the back of my hand. "Sorry. That felt good," I say, smiling shyly. "Tasted good, too."

Sébastien goes to a garbage can to throw the empty bottle away. I watch him walk back. Deadly half smile pulling up the left corner of his mouth, hands carelessly in his pockets, hair loosely down. He's animalistic and primitively regal, like the ruler of the animal kingdom stalking his prey, watching it cower before he takes its life. My palms begin to sweat. I'm dizzy, weak on my knees. Maybe I had too much champagne to drink?

No, it's him.

Yes, it's definitely him.

"La Bohème" is playing in the background, the famous tune floating out of the windows where the party is still going strong. Cars fly by. The Eiffel Tower watches us. Some pedestrians walk past.

He stops in front of me, shrugs out of his tuxedo jacket and drapes it over my bare shoulders protectively. I slip my arms in the sleeves of the jacket, enjoying the traces of warmth left over from his body and the lingering smell of his cologne. His eyes on me. The way he's looking at me. It's all that matters.

"I can't offer you a dance in the rain right now. But, how about in the moonlight?" he says huskily, the lamppost bathing him in an amber haze.

Oh, Sébastien. "You were paying attention ..."

"Of course, I was. When it comes to you, I always am." An easy grin slowly spreads on his handsome face. "Now, shall we?"

My hand trembles as he takes it and places it on his chest, close to where his heart is. He wraps an arm around my waist and pulls me flush against him. A gasp escapes my lips, a shiver of pleasure spreading through me.

A ball of nerves, I try smiling and making a joke out of the situation. "If I step on you, I apologize in advance. I'm terrible at this. Two-left-feet Val here. Once a guy told me that I looked prettier sitting down than—"

"I highly doubt that. Remember? The kitchen. I saw you dancing."

"T-that was different. I didn't—"

"Valentina ..."

"Oh, yes. Right. We're dancing."

"More like trying to." He chuckles when I whack him on the shoulder, the sound soft and toe-curling. "Come, put your feet on top of mine."

"What? No, your shoes will be ruined."

"C'est la vie. Enough stalling, Valentina. Dance with me." He lifts me so my feet are on top of his feet, and begins to sway.

"Are you okay?" I ask, wincing a little, imagining that this must be painful for him.

"Never better," he whispers close to my ear, tightening his grip around me. "I've got you, ma petite chouette."

I've got you. Simple words, but how safe do they make one feel.

I let my gaze roam over his features while getting lost in the heady sensation of being in his arms. Sébastien is like the sun. Dark without him, and bright, so bright whenever he's near you. He can be blinding, but what does it matter when your body is burning once again?

And under the moonlight and the stars as our witnesses, we move slowly, effortlessly. There's no rush. No room for thought. Just pleasure. The world could be falling apart, and it wouldn't matter. I lean my head on his strong shoulder, smelling his scent of man and smoke and champagne, filling my lungs until every pore of mine is drowning in him. He moves closer, resting his cheek on top of my head, taking a deep breath. And baby, it's good. We become two bodies slow dancing in a wildfire. If there's nothing left of me after this, it will all be worth it because, for the first time in a very long time, I remember.

I remember what it is to feel alive.

"Ready?"

"Hmm?"

"Do you trust me?" he asks throatily, tightening his grip around my waist, pulling me closer to him.

I blink a couple times, still in a daze. However, the answer jumps out of me. "Yes."

"Good."

Sébastien takes me by surprise when he bends me backward over his arm, whisking me into an extravagant dip that is close to the ground. A shriek of shock turns into laughter and more laughter. And then laughter turns into a silence full of meanings that can't be spoken. My heart kicks into overdrive, an invisible chord pulling me toward him.

He kisses my forehead, chuckling ruefully. "It seems we have an audience."

"What?" I ask, disoriented by the sensation of his lips on my skin.

Straightening with me in his arms, Sébastien winks before twirling me one last time. The movement grand, elaborate. I squeal with happiness as he catches me by the hips and brings our bodies flush against each other.

The sound of mad clapping erupts somewhere from our right. I let go of him and turn in the direction of the small group of people watching us. Heart soaring and feeling silly, I reach for the edges of my dress, grabbing them between my fingers on each hand, pull the skirt out to each side, and accord them with a very pretty, ladylike curtsy. Out of the corner of my eye, I see Sébastien bowing to our audience, which makes them lose their minds. Our gazes meet briefly over the sounds of clapping and some catcalling. I smile. He smiles. And the world disappears around us.

I'm falling for him.

The thought doesn't come as a surprise. It's more like opening my eyes and seeing the blue sky for the first time in a very long time.

CHAPTER FIFTEEN

Burying my face in the pillow, I avoid opening my eyes for a little while longer. I wiggle my toes relishing the sensation of my skin against silk sheets. My entire body exhales in pleasure as memories begin to replay like a broken record of my favorite album in my mind. Was any of it real or just a lovely, lovely dream made out of wishful thinking?

But it must have happened. Because there's this lightness in my chest. I feel like I can fly. I want to get up and jump on the bed like a toddler. Laugh and laugh until my stomach hurts and I can't breathe. Hold onto this feeling and live forever just like this.

Letting out a sigh, I flip on my back and open my eyes. My gaze lands on the crystal chandelier and the rainbow of light reflected by each piece of glass. I blink a couple of times before reaching for my phone to look at the time. It's eight in the morning, then I focus on the date.

It's Tuesday.

Another kind of excitement flows through me. I'm supposed to be at the flower shop in two hours. About to get out of bed, I hear the doorbell ring. Frowning, I reach for my cardigan and put it over my silk nightgown before I open the door to find a young deliveryman holding a large plastic bag. The smell of butter flows out of it. Curiosity disperses the last traces of sleep from my mind. Helmet in hand, he smiles as he hands me a note.

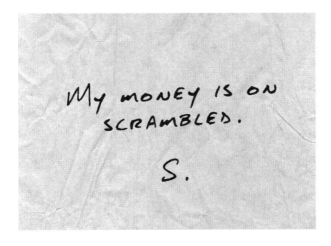

My money is on
scrambled.

S.

I take the bag from the guy and go in search of my wallet. I tip him and shut the door behind me. I raise the expensive stationery to my lips and kiss it as though it's Sébastien's lips. After placing the note carefully in the front pocket of my cardigan, I walk to the kitchen, place the bag on the counter, and take out multiple plastic containers filled with food. I take off the lid of each one of them to find eggs prepared every which way: a frittata, an omelet, over easy, sunny side up, and the list goes on. An explosion of pleasure and delight bursts from somewhere deep inside me. *Oh, Sébastien. You silly, wonderful man.*

Out of the shower, I get ready in no time. I skip the blow dryer and let my hair dry naturally. *Embrace the curl, the inner rebel inside me jokes.* Summer, flowery dress. Check. Flats. Check. Perfume and lip-gloss. Check. Glasses. Check. Ready to conquer the world? Abso-fucking-lutely check.

On the way to the flower shop, I discover new smells. New sounds. The soundtrack of the city becomes a beautiful harmony to match its rhythm. I take a deep breath as I trace the flowerbeds lining an iron gate with the tips of my fingers while walking past it. The silky smoothness of the petals reminds me of Sébastien's touch. I wonder where's the guilt, the shame. But my heart remains blind, quiet to all of it. I try to picture William, but the eyes of my mind show me a man and a woman dancing under the moonlight to "La Bohème" as each step they take slowly illuminates every dark corner of her life.

Shaking my head, I push thoughts of William out of my mind. I will deal with the mess I've made when the time comes. The day will eventually come when the consequences of my actions catch up to me.

But today isn't that day.

So I turn my back on reality. Wanting to enjoy this borrowed rose-colored dream for as long as I can.

When I arrive at the flower shop, I find Mr. Lemaire already inside waiting for me. He greets me with a tentative smile and a dictionary of French to English in hand. I laugh.

"It seems like we had the same idea." I pull out of my leather bag a dictionary of English to French and place it on the counter. Mr. Lemaire focuses on the book and nods, his weathered blue eyes twinkling with good humor.

I give my head a tiny shake and smile at him, thinking that it's time to set this place straight. Placing my hands on my hips, I scan my surroundings. *Hmm.* The flowers need watering and some trimming. Shelves are covered in dust. The floor needs a good sweep and mopping. The windows need attention too. I should be daunted by the amount of work ahead of me, but that's the last thing on my mind. In fact, I've never been more ready in my life. Every part of me is vibrating with vigor and excitement.

I notice Mr. Lemaire observing me with curiosity and interest, probably trying to figure me out. I can almost picture what he sees. A woman more suited for The Ritz than at a decaying store swimming in dust. But the woman he sees is not who I am. It's who I thought I needed to be, but not anymore. With each second that I spend in this place, that I spend in Paris, I'm more myself than I ever was in my cavernous house in Greenwich.

I point toward the back of the store and then mimic the movements of sweeping the floor. Mr. Lemaire frowns, confusion embedded in the lines of his forehead. If this were a cartoon, this is where he'd scratch his head as a big question mark appeared above him. I laugh, reaching for my dictionary sitting on the glass. After finding the word I'm searching for, I put down the book and look at him.

Our eyes meet. "*Moi.*" I point toward me. "*Balai,*" I say, pretending to hold a broom in my hand.

"Ohh!" He nods. "*Aimerais-tu faire le par terre,*" he says.

I'm not really sure what he's saying, but I nod nonetheless, enjoying myself regardless of the very obvious language barrier between us. He gestures for me to follow him to the back of the store, and there he hands me a book with pictures of flower arrangements.

What?

How did we go from brooms to books? Did I use the wrong word?

Confused, I stare at the book in my hands when I hear Mr. Lemaire chuckling. Meeting his gaze, he's watching me with an impish light in his eyes while holding a broom in his hand. Oh, he got me, and he got me good.

Laughing, I give him the book and reach for the broom. "Merci." Mr. Lemaire, you naughty man.

The day passes in a blur. My soul dances in a swirling room made out of new experiences: the sensation of dirt beneath my fingers. Sweat across my forehead. The quiet, seldom laughter of Mr. Lemaire at seeing me tending to the flowers as though they are little children. Misunderstandings turning into more laughter. A quiet lunch sitting on the bench outside the store next to Mr. Lemaire who doesn't say much because he doesn't have to. I take my flats off, placing them on the ground next to me, wiggling my painted toes. The warm breeze kisses our skin, making our hair twirl in the wind. A sense of accomplishment takes over me, and my goodness, it is good.

When it's time to close, Mr. Lemaire pats my cheek with a timeworn hand as his eyes hold mine. I wish I knew the words to thank him for what he's done for me today, the gift he's given me, but I don't think I could ever find the right ones. We say goodbye until tomorrow.

Feeling like I'm at the top of the world, I rush home because I want to tell Sébastien about my day. I want to see him. Spend time with him. Watch the same wayward lock of hair fall over his one eye.

I stop at my place to pick up a bottle of champagne. Excitement pumps through my veins as I skip the elevator and take the stairs to his floor instead. Once I'm standing in front of his door, I take a deep calming breath and ring the doorbell twice before I have a chance to change my mind. There's a part of me that wants to flee, afraid that he'll think I'm being too forward. But the other tells me to chill, that I'm not doing anything wrong.

He opens the door. I raise the bottle and smile invitingly. "About that drink I owe you ..."

Sébastien grins crookedly, scratching the back of his neck

as his gaze lands on the champagne. My God. It's like he's a gift sent from the underworld to show and taunt us with the kind of pleasures one would find if we gave into temptation and sinned. "What's the special occasion?"

"We're celebrating."

"Oh yeah? What are we celebrating?

"Life."

CHAPTER SIXTEEN

Valentina

I SPEND MY MORNINGS helping Mr. Lemaire in the flower shop, and little by little the store comes back to life. The dust is replaced by various blooms, and more customers walk in. Even Mr. Lemaire laughs more; we both do. My French hasn't really improved, but with the help of Sébastien, who stops once in a while to have lunch with us, we're able to communicate better and smooth out the bumps created by the language barrier.

And it's wonderful. To find a purpose. To be able to look at yourself in the mirror and be proud of the woman staring back at you.

Before I know it, I've been in Paris for a few months. William doesn't call anymore, and I've stopped expecting him to. And each day that passes, Sébastien embeds himself deeper in the DNA of my life, of my soul. From the first moment I laid my eyes on him, he's slowly filled my world with colors I'd forgotten existed. And now it's bursting with them.

Walks along the river on starry nights with him by my side while I balance myself on the ledge, arms extended, heart glowing. Sharing anecdotes in hidden cafés as we get drunk on wine, on food, and I get drunk on him. Dancing into the wee hours of the morning while Sébastien teaches me how to tango along the banks of the Seine.

Laughing at everything and nothing at all.

Thoughts of him keep intruding my mind. They make me blush and awaken my body with a hunger deep in my core that I haven't felt in a very long time. Sometimes late at night, I reach under the covers, spread my legs apart, and fuck myself with my fingers while wishing it was his hardness inside me. I lick my lips, and I wish it were his tongue. Rub my nipples and imagine it's his mouth. I reach for a pillow, pretending it's his body, and then I come, whispering his name into an empty room like a prayer or an invocation.

It's as though God has said, "Here, child, I give you the food for your starving soul. The music to fill the silence. The sun to warm you. The moon, the stars to show you the way. But be careful. Don't be greedy. Too much of one thing can never be good."

But I am greedy.

I keep borrowing more and more time with him, knowing full well that the clock is ticking. The sand running out of the hourglass. So I continue to live in my little bubble, praying that the tomorrows keep coming as I fall and fall, and that's all I can do.

CHAPTER SEVENTEEN

William

Reclining my back on the leather chair, I stare at the ceiling while bouncing a baseball against it. In the dark, the thumping sounds are soothing. The place is empty except for the cleaning crew and me. The lines ringing nonstop outside my office have been replaced by Latin music booming from a portable player outside in the hall.

I should get out of here, but my pathetic grandmother has gotten to me, ruining what was shaping up to be a perfect day. The returns were looking good. It felt like we were finally getting a break after a string of bad investments and even worse returns. But then her visit came.

Loretta Fitzpatrick, the matriarch who holds the keys to all the money I desperately need, barged into my office without giving a damn that I was in the middle of a meeting. Larry and a few of the traders could go to hell for all she cared. Cane in hand, pearls worn like artillery, she came into the room ready for battle. Gone were the kind hellos and kisses on cheeks. Her grandson had disappointed her, and she was letting him know of her displeasure.

"William," she said coldly as way of greeting, giving her head a slight nod and ignoring the rest of the men.

My secretary stood on the threshold of the door, guilt and fear implanted on her features. "Sir, she wouldn't wait until the meeting was over."

My grandmother didn't dignify her with an answer. Instead, she focused all of her attention on me. "Please, dismiss your meeting. I'd like to have a word with you in private," she paused, her shrewd blue eyes burning holes in me, "unless, of course, you are far too busy for me."

Sarcasm dripped from her words because she knew that no one, not even me, would dare to deny her anything. Least of all, when she had come all the way from Greenwich for this meeting. Loretta Fitzpatrick was used to ruling an empire with an iron fist, and she led her private life in the same manner. Nothing but perfection would do. My poor grandfather had no choice but to sit back and watch her do his job for him. Consequently, he drank and whored until his death, not that I blamed him one bit.

It could also be said that she expected the same perfection in her children and grandchildren. My adoptive father, an only child from an unhappy marriage, killed himself and his lover in a boating accident. Loretta blamed my adoptive mother for his death, saying that it was her detachment and coldness that had driven him into the arms of another woman. Of course, she didn't know that her precious son enjoyed hitting his wife and children after polishing off a particularly remarkable bottle of scotch or when in one of his darker moods. The sick motherfucker got a kick out of hearing us cry or seeing technicolor bruises on our skin. And after he'd left Gwyneth and I black and blue, he would grab my mother by the hair, dragging her to their room and finishing her on the bed. The more she resisted, the more he enjoyed it. Sometimes he even made us watch, taking a sick pleasure in our disgust and fear. The one time I tried to fight him, he broke my mother's wrist. An eye for an eye, he had said. I hated him. The day he died was the happiest day of my life.

I never forgave my grandmother for choosing to be blind when all the signs were there, and for making our mother feel more unworthy than she already did. Soon after, she passed away of cancer. And as I stood over the hole in the ground, her casket being lowered to the ground along with the remnants of my soul, I made a vow to myself. I would never allow myself to feel. Amongst flower arrangements and a sea of people dressed in black, I raised a hand to my chest right where my heart should've been and felt nothing.

Then my eyes had landed on my grandmother who remained untouched, aloof, and hatred filled me once again. All I wanted was for her to die and leave me the hell alone along with the fortune that was rightfully mine.

"Please excuse us," I said, dismissing the meeting.

As the men shuffled out of my office, my gaze found my grandmother's and the old hate came back, ramming its horns deep in my chest. When the last person stepped out and closed the door behind him, we stood facing each other surrounded by silence.

"To what do I owe this pleasure?" I asked charmingly.

Loretta closed the space between us and sat down on the chair directly facing my desk. She was pushing ninety, but you would never know it by the way she held herself. Ramrod straight like the cane in her hands. Regal like a queen. "You know exactly why I am here. Mrs. Croft told me about your failed trip. Why is Valentina still in Paris?"

I shrugged carelessly, not surprised that the housekeeper would keep her informed about the state of my marriage. Keeping tabs on us was her sole purpose in the house when she wasn't pretending to work. And I couldn't fire her without pissing grandmother off.

"I guess she felt like sightseeing."

"What do you take me for? Your lovesick wife? You've disappointed her again, haven't you?"

I remained silent while waiting for her to continue punishing me with her words, not that they could cause me any harm. She couldn't touch me. No one could.

"I was sure you were different from all the men in the family, but it seems I was mistaken. Is there someone else again?"

I shook my head, loosening my tie. "No one. I promised you I was done with all of that after the first time."

She eyed me up and down, suspicion marking her every move. Maybe she knew I was full of shit after all. "Good. I meant what I said the last time it happened. Both your grandfather and father disappointed me. And if you do too, if that girl files for divorce, I will disinherit you. It's simple. I'm tired of our last name being associated with that kind of vulgarity."

My grandmother, it seemed, wanted to make a point. And when she did, she did not give a damn about the consequences. And there was no fucking way in hell I would let her take that away from me. I hadn't put up with her all this time for nothing. That inheritance was mine.

"I understand," I said softly.

"Excellent. I trust you'll know what to do."

I stood and made my way to her side to try to help her stand, but she dismissed my assistance with the wave of a hand. Slowly but surely she made her way to the door and opened it. Waiting outside in the hall was good old Don—her trusted driver. He went to her immediately offering his arm. As she placed a wrinkled hand on his forearm covered in a black suit, she turned to look at me, ready to fire her loaded words one last time, "Don't disappoint me, William."

She left without taking another glance at her disobedient grandchild. And as I watched her walk away from me, an intense dislike bordering on hate for Valentina spread like black ink inside me. Why couldn't she do what I wanted? Why did she have to stay there?

I planned our trip to Paris as a way to appease her. She always got difficult and testy around our anniversary. But a last minute meeting came up, and Brooke wanted me to take her away for a night. After that, I lost interest in going. I figured Valentina would come back on her own. I never thought that she would choose that moment to finally grow a backbone. Like always, Valentina's timing was just fucking perfect.

Angrily shoving those thoughts aside, I get up, letting the ball bounce on the carpeted floor, forgotten, and stand in front of the floor to ceiling window behind my desk. Rubbing the back of my neck, I stare at the skyline of the city. The lights are everywhere. Everything appears to be pulsing with life—that is everything on the other side of this glass wall.

I chuckle, thinking of the naïve boy I once was. Before I discovered that evil lurked beneath the most perfect façades. I often wonder what would have become of me had my father turned out to be a decent man. Would my life be any different? What if I had been adopted by a different family?

There was a time when I had hope.

Hope came in the shape of a tall girl-woman with wild hair the color of milk chocolate. When I first met Valentina, I saw someone full of dreams, full of life. I took one look into her guileless eyes and felt that maybe the world wasn't such a shitty place. I wanted to believe what she believed in. I wanted to be the man she thought I was because that man was good and worthy. Unsullied. Was I in love with her? No, but I wanted to be. And for a while, I fooled myself into thinking that I had finally found peace.

But like all fantasies built upon shaky walls, the cracks soon started to show, slowly crumbling down and turning to dust. I wanted Valentina to save me from myself, and for a while I'd thought she could, but I was wrong. No one could save me. So hope contorted itself into despair, marring the beauty of the promised land within my reach.

Her love began to choke me. I couldn't be near her without feeling impatience and disappointment. Disappointment because she wasn't the woman I thought she was. She was weak, needy— her love for me made her pathetic. It was like a noose tied around my neck depriving me of air.

Valentina. Once my hope, she was now the one who could ruin everything that I've worked damn hard to achieve. And there's no fucking way I'm going to let her.

A few doors down, I hear the faint sound of Larry's grandfather clock announcing the hour. It's past midnight. I pack my things, go down to the garage, get in my car, and head home.

But even on my drive across town, I can't stop thinking about it all. My family. My past. My present. Valentina. Tightening my hold on the steering wheel, I change lanes and head somewhere else.

Brooke takes my cock in her hand and brings it between her legs, rubbing her clit with it. Sitting up on the bed with my back reclined against the frame, I watch her magnificent tits as she pushes me inside of her, coating my cock with her desire. And unlike my frigid wife who I basically have to coerce to have sex with me, this woman is made to fuck.

I circle her waist with my fingers as I guide the punishing rhythm of our coupling. It's hard and fast. She slaps me when I lean over and bite her tit, making sure to draw blood. Darkness blacks out my conscience. I flip her onto her back and enter her cunt in one punishing thrust enjoying her cries of pain and need.

When she begins to fight me, scratching my face and my arms, my hands go to her delicate neck. Tightening my hold around the fragile length, I watch her trying to take her next breath while my cock continues to piston in and out of her mercilessly—viciously—fucking the life out of her. Our bodies are covered in sweat. The room smells like our dirty souls. And I fucking love it.

She comes first, her eyes closing as her cunt spasms intensely around my cock. When I can't hold it any longer, I pull out of her and spill myself on her stomach. I throw back my head, a shout torn from my chest, the intensity of the orgasm blinding.

I'm now lying in bed as I watch her naked form step out of the bathroom. While she towels her wet hair, I observe the red marks I've left behind on her body, perversely enjoying them.

"I might not be able to see you for sometime."

She tilts her head to the side making her blond hair fall over her left shoulder. "Your wife is back?"

I shake my head, the anger and resentment that disappeared as soon I got here stir awake inside me. "Loretta has given me an ultimatum."

"She did?" she asks, raising an eyebrow. "What is it?"

"Don't worry your pretty little head. I've got it under control. Come over here."

She discards the towel on the floor before joining me on the bed and straddling my lap. I raise a hand to trace my fingerprints on her neck. A depraved pleasure coats my senses. "Did I hurt you?"

Brooke shakes her head. "You're one sick motherfucker, you know?"

I chuckle wryly before remembering my grandmother's warning and sober up. "I'm going to miss this," I say, running the back of my fingers along her tits to her stomach and down to her hot, wet pussy.

Closing her eyes, she moans when I spread her apart and rub her clit with my thumb. Her hands go to my shoulders for support as she begins to grind herself on me. "You make it sound final ..." she gasps when I impale her with four of my fingers. "What are you planning to do?"

I kiss her instead of giving her an answer.

CHAPTER EIGHTEEN
Sébastien

You're my midnight thought and my 11:11 wish.

THE AIR SMELLS LIKE sweet grass, and the sun's bright and warm with not a cloud in the sky. I stand on the veranda transfixed, watching the outline of a woman running and laughing as a group of kids chase her. Lips wide, her unruly curls flow down her back with a dandelion flower crown sitting unevenly on top of her head. She's wearing a dress more suited for a day at the beach than an exclusive diplomatic party at a chateau outside Paris, but one look at her, and you wouldn't give a damn whether she wore a sack of potatoes or a ball gown. You wouldn't be able to take your eyes off of her. And it isn't because she's the most striking woman in the place. There are others with far more classical features than hers. But none of them can hold a candle to her. She reminds me of the sea: untamed, unpredictable, but beautiful, so damn beautiful.

Valentina glances in my direction, eyes shining, an inviting, healthy blush on her cheeks, and waves enthusiastically before the pack of brats tackle her with hugs. I bury my hands in the front pockets of my slacks, enjoying the show, and laugh at the sight. Even the kids have lost their heart to her.

"It's really lovely to hear that sound once again ..."

Absorbed in the tableau unfolding in front of me, I'd failed to notice my cousin coming to stand next to me. Tearing my eyes away from Valentina, I focus on Sophie. Many say she's the beauty of the family, and I have to agree. "What's that?"

"You. Laughing."

I nod. "There are a lot of kids here."

"Oh, you know Jack. He must always invite everyone who's remotely associated with the Embassy." She studies Valentina. "They all seem to really like her." She lifts a flute of champagne to her lips, takes a sip. "Be careful, Sébastien."

"What do you mean?" I frown, not liking where this is going. "Nothing's happened."

"Not yet," she adds, watching me from the corner of her eye. "Listen, Sebs, I really like Valentina, too. I truly think she's the perfect woman for you. Her one, maybe only, flaw is that she's married."

"I know."

"You think you know, babe. But you've never been married. You can't erase the years they've been together. And the moment you try to make her choose between her husband and you, you'll lose her." She pauses, measuring her next sentence. "For all you know, it could be another rough patch."

About a week ago, Sophie and Jack came over for dinner at my apartment. Valentina was there. Conversation flowed like the wine. One glass turned into five or eight bottles. Before I knew it, Valentina opened up about her marriage. There was no anger anymore. She didn't even blame William. It was as though she had finally come to terms with the state of whatever was left of it. And the bastard in me was happy.

"Her husband doesn't deserve her."

"That's not for you to decide." She pats my chest. "Be smart. Don't take it any further."

I shake my head, reach for her hand, covering it with mine. "I don't think I can quit her."

"Have you even tried?"

"I don't want to."

"You're fucked then, handsome. Just remember, she and her husband are unfinished business."

Jealousy makes me see fucking red. "What the fuck is that supposed to mean?"

"You know exactly what it means. It's not over until it's over."
She pats my jaw tenderly before walking away to join the rest of
her guests.

Unsettled by Sophie's warning, I go in search of Valentina.
The need to be with her corrodes my bones. As soon as I spot her
sitting on the grass with little Jack on her lap and the other kids
around her, I'm calm once again. Fuck her husband. If he truly
loved her, he would have been here the next day. If Valentina were
mine, I would have moved heaven and earth to get to her. Because
when you finally find something worth living for, you fight until
there isn't one more drop of blood left in you.

As I approach their spot, the anger and fear gradually slip from
my pores. I don't have the answers to her marriage, only she does,
but we will figure it out. She remains unaware of my existence, so
I hang back, reclining my shoulder on the trunk of a tree. I listen
to her soft voice as my eyes devour her. The fabric clings to her
slim curves as the wind blows past her, molding onto her like a
second skin.

"Once upon a time there was a sad king of a vast land where
midnight was eternal. Children grew up not knowing what the sun
or a morning sky looked like. It was also said that when the king
was angry, rain and howling winds would follow, shaking their
homes with its angry power."

"He sounds scary," a little boy says and hugs himself.

"He wasn't scary, Tobias. He was just lonely and very cranky.
That's why he scowled all the time." Valentina shakes her head
and smiles.

"He sounds like my father," Jack says, giggling.

Valentina laughs, and the sound is like music to my fucking
ears. "Anyway, the king was feared by all, tenants, servants,
and neighboring rulers alike. He was known to be ruthless and
unfeeling."

"What did he look like?"

"Hmm." She taps her chin seemingly thinking of her answer.

"A bear!" Jack orders.

"A horse?" another girl offers shyly.

"Yes! How clever you both are." Valentina smiles encouragingly
at the kids, and Jack grows about five inches with manly pride. She
glances around her engrossed audience and lowers her voice. "It
was said that he had the face of a bear and the body of a horse. His

subjects dreaded to come into contact with him for they believed that he could turn them into stone. So the poor king lived in seclusion in his big castle at the top of the highest hill."

"That is very sad," my niece Isabella says. "Living all by himself."

"Bet you daddy would like it," Jack interjects, making Valentina chuckle. "He's allergic to people, you know."

"Oh, I know!" Isabella exclaims. "He needed a beautiful princess with a flower crown just like you to kiss him and turn him into a handsome king."

Pushing myself away from the trunk, I stroll toward the circle of children and the minx at its center. "Now the story gets more interesting ..."

Valentina's eyes dance with laughter as she holds my gaze. "No. Sadly, it wasn't in the cards for him."

"More's the pity." I cross my arms, raising an eyebrow. "What happens with this scowling monster?"

"He wasn't a monster. Just misunderstood. Now, if you would be kind enough as to remain quiet so I can finish the story, I'd be forever grateful."

I nod graciously as a smile tugs the corners of my lips. Valentina spreads her skirt carefully and hugs little Jack in her arms once more. Lucky boy. "Where was I? Oh, yeah. One day, a gypsy girl in a blue caravan stopped outside the castle."

"Was she beautiful?" the same little blond girl from before asks.

"Of course she was. They always are," an older girl interrupted.

"Does the king fall in love with the gypsy?"

"Ew, no!" the boys shout in dislike almost unanimously. *Poor kids. If they only knew ...*

We lose the kids' attention as they start to laugh and fight amongst themselves. Not that it matters. She stands up, brushing the grass and dirt off her skirt, and closes the space between us. An indecent smile on her wide mouth, that damn dimple that drives me to distraction peeking, she comes to me as though she's a virgin ready to be sacrificed to the gods. Taunting me. Intoxicating me. A gust of wind blows past her as it sends her hair flying in all directions, making her dress dance in the air.

She's now standing in front of me. "You look familiar. Have we met before?"

"I certainly hope so," I drawl, tucking a strand of hair behind her ear.

"You know, Sophie's right, you do touch me whenever you feel like it," she teases.

"And yet it's still not enough."

Valentina lowers her face, blushing a little, but not before I see her smiling. Out of the corner of my eye, I notice heavy-looking clouds move across the sky, covering the sun. The smell of rain filters through my nose. Trees sway back and forth in the breeze. And then it comes. The rain. Soft. Gentle. Fresh on our skin.

She wipes a raindrop off of my forehead, concern written on her features. "We should go inside."

I nod, trying to remain calm. Hoping that it stays just like this. No thunder. No memories. She reaches for my hand and entwines her fingers with mine, the gesture natural like her hand has always belonged there. We run until we reach a large tree. We are standing under its shelter when an image flashes right in front of my eyes. It's of an older man watching his kids play outside in the rain. Secluded in the safety of his living room, he wishes he could join them, but he can't. He's too afraid. So he must be content to just sit back and see his life pass by.

I squeeze her hand. "I don't want to run anymore." Life is already too short to spend it watching it from the sidelines.

"Are you sure?"

As kids and adults run past us, trying to avoid getting wet, we remain in our spot. It's time to face my demons straight on. What's the worst that can happen? That they take me back to hell? It's not like I haven't been there before. I let my gaze fall on our hands, thinking, *and I came back. I survived.*

"Yes, I'm sure."

I step out of the shelter of the tree, close my eyes, tilt my head back, and feel the rain as it cleanses me from the inside out. There are no grand gestures. No magic words to make the pain disappear. But today I fight back. Today, I choose life.

I open my eyes, focus on her gorgeous face, and grin. "If I remember correctly, you once told me you wanted to dance in the rain. Well, ma petite chouette. How about a dance?"

"What?" Her eyes widen in surprise, but she smiles nonetheless. "Now?"

"Yeah, why the fuck not?"

"You're crazy," she says laughingly, but she comes running toward me anyway. And in that moment, she is as lovely as she is free. "But so am I it seems."

I wrap my arm around her waist, pulling her closer to me. Desire, hunger, and yearning for her reverberate like an echo within me. "Ready, ma petite chouette?"

Her own arms go around my neck, beaming. "Never been more ready."

We begin to move under the rain. Our clothes are soaked. But none of it matters. Victor Hugo once said *La vie est une fleur dont l'amour est le miel.* Life is a flower of which love is the honey.

The man was onto something.

Ever since Valentina came into my life, I knew I had no chance against her. I was fucked the second she walked into the gallery and life threw her my way. Now that I've had a taste of a life with her in it, the one I led before wouldn't be enough for me. I want her to dance for me naked under the stars. I want to make love to her as her hair falls on my face and her slim body takes me in over and over again. I want her to show me how to live life without fear—without restrictions.

Sophie once told me that love doesn't divide. It multiplies. That Poppy would have wanted me to find love again, to move on, to live. But my heart remained shut. Silent. Frozen. Unmoved by the parade of women that came into my life, adorning my bed and keeping my body warm every night.

But then I met Valentina.

And the world was right again.

I will always love Poppy. Mourn for her and our unborn child. Nobody can replace her. Because it isn't a competition. I don't need to love one more than the other. But as I stare at Valentina, feel my arms around her, her heart drumming against mine, I finally understand what Sophie meant when she said love doesn't divide.

It multiplies.

As I lay my eyes on Valentina, never breaking our gaze, I willingly jump down a precipice. Some people call it insanity. I call it love.

She's mine, I tell myself.

But for how much longer, another voice answers.

CHAPTER NINETEEN
Valentina

WE'RE NOW STANDING outside my apartment. Lingering. Not ready for the night to be over. Not ready to say goodbye.

"Thank you for today, Sébastien. I had a great time." I should invite him in, but something inside me forbids it.

"Don't mention it."

I point behind me, toward the door. "I need to ... uh ... it might be too late for a nightcap but—"

"It's better this way." He gives his head a gentle shake. "I'm going to be responsible and do the right thing and go."

I stare at my feet, unable to look him in the eye because I'm afraid I'll beg him to stay. "Please."

Before I know what's happening, he places a finger under my chin and makes me look at him. The small hairs on the back of my neck stand. "You know what I keep wishing for?"

I shake my head.

"For another life, in another universe, with you by my side. Now go inside and close the door."

Without asking any questions, I do as he says. Inside the apartment, I shut the door behind me and recline my head against it as I take a deep breath. It's better this way, I tell myself, but I might as well be talking to deaf ears for all the good it does. Every part of my soul screams to go after him, but I can't.

A sigh escapes my lips as my sight lands on the mirror hung on the wall to my left. I stare at my reflection. Gone is the flawless woman whose husband didn't want her, who hadn't felt enough in a long time. Instead, I see someone with fire in her eyes. She smiles, and you can see traces of the woman she used to be. The one who wasn't afraid to jump in puddles and cry in coffee-shops, and it's because of Sébastien. He's made me remember how it feels to be me.

What are you doing here? The voice inside my head asks. *Go after him.*

What am I going to say to him?

Does it matter? Go!

My heart begins to pump hard as the need to see him again comes over me. Throwing caution to the wind, I open the door, ready to rush out in search of him, but I stop frozen in place.

Sébastien is standing outside my apartment with a hand raised in the air, appearing like he was about to knock on the door. I pause to soak up the hard lines of his face, thirstily drinking them in.

"You're still here," I say feebly, feeling like a bomb of butterflies just went off inside me.

The sleeves of his white shirt are rolled up to his elbows. Feet spread apart. He lowers his hand, a faint, rueful smile plays on the corners of his mouth. "I'm still here."

I stand there and forget about heartache and repercussions. Because I'm selfish. Flawed. Hurt. Tired, so tired, of living in the dark. I want to *know, feel* what it's like to be bathed in his light, even if it's for a short time. I want to pretend we're just two people who have finally found each other in this vast world.

"Why?"

"Because you are."

He steps forward, or I do. It doesn't matter. Our bodies collide as he buries his hands in my hair, pulling me closer to him as though he's trying to meld us into one. We get lost in a moment that takes us to a place where the past and future are irrelevant—they don't exist. And it feels a little like falling. A lot like flying. Crashing on the ground. Dancing in the clouds. A cage and an open sky. The light of a thousand lamps illuminating the dark night.

He lowers his face and traces my jawline, my cheekbones—

everywhere—with his lips, his hands, showering me with urgent, punishing kisses that leave a searing trail behind them. "Tell me to go," he urges, his voice vibrating with intensity. "Tell me to leave you alone."

"I can't." My entire body shakes with the enormity of what's happening. *Finally, finally, it cries.* The feel of his lips on my skin drives me mad as want, yearning, need all morph into one. "I can't lie to you."

"You must. Don't you see? Can't you see how much I want you? How much I need you? I can't fucking breathe when you're around." Sébastien's hands tremble as his gaze falls to my lips then looks up, meeting my eyes again. He pauses, his hold turning intense, deep passion vibrating in his voice. "I have no right to touch you, to crave you as much as I do, but God help me, I can't stop. I've tried to do the right thing, but I can't anymore. You're all I can think about. I feel like I'm going mad if I don't see you, if I'm not touching you. Yet when you're here with me, it's never enough. Not fucking enough."

Then he presses his mouth to mine. And it's a savage exchange. A pent up beast finally let loose, kissing me as madly and wantonly as I feel. We go to war. No idea how we make it inside my apartment. He pushes me or I push him against the door. It doesn't matter. I laugh, he laughs. We are all tongues and mouths and hands. He kisses me like he's dying and my lips are his last breath. It's a kiss that rearranges the stars in my own little galaxy, setting my life in a new course, changing my destiny. And if I crash and burn like a falling star, what does it matter when for this brief instant I'm in his arms? For the first time in a very long time, there isn't ice inside of me. Instead, there's a bright, hot, blazing fire.

I should ask him to stop, but I can't bring myself to utter one word. Instead, I let his sweet breath inebriate me as his touch crumbles my defenses along with my reason. I begin to shake with warring shame and pleasure when his fingers slide the straps of my sundress off my shoulders, slowly exposing my skin to him. The back of his fingers caress the curve of my shoulder, tracing the goose bumps now covering my skin.

"Jesus fucking Christ, Valentina. What are you doing to me? I'm jealous of the sun because it touches your skin when I can't. I'm jealous of every man that came before me," he breathes between lovely, lovely kisses that take and demand and mark me as his. Sébastien grabs my ass, desperation making his movements forceful. He pulls me close, grinding his growing hardness against me. I moan as he imprints the hot outline of his cock between my legs, showing me how much he wants me. Urgency and desire take over, making every movement frenzied, more needy, more, more, and more.

Sébastien pushes my dress down, exposing my small breasts to his view. I know I should feel some sort of shame, but my head and pride are gone. "Darkness is around me until I see you. Then it's colors. Bright, bright colors I can't describe," I say shakily as my body screams for him, wantonly begging for him to take me. A moan passes my lips when Sébastien buries his face in my breasts, sucking my pebbled nipples into his mouth, rolling the tips with his tongue, sending shooting stars through me. It all becomes too much, too intense, too beautiful.

His mouth is everywhere on me, etching himself deeper on my skin. Lowering his hand, he slides it under the material of my dress, running his fingers against the gusset of my wet lacy thong. He teases me. He torments me. Cursing, he slips the thin, wet fabric to the side and finds my clit swollen for him. He rubs it nice and slow as he tears moans out of me, making every cell sing.

"Fuck ... that sound is so damn addictive."

I bury my hands in his hair and throw my head back, combusting from within as he plays me like a maestro, creating a harmonious symphony with my savaged body. I lick my dry lips, swallowing hard, trying to breathe, but my lungs are all out of air. And when I don't think I can handle any more of his beautiful torture, he sinks two fingers deep inside me where I need him the most, where I burn for him the most. He begins to pump in and out of me mercilessly, driving me closer to a blinding, exploding climax. His kisses and touches turn more demanding, and I give him everything he asks for. But when he unzips his pants, and I feel the head of his cock against my entrance, everything is brought to a screeching halt.

"No ... I can't ... stop ..." I push him away yet hold onto the front of his shirt, afraid to let him go. "Not that."

He curses and lifts his burning eyes to me, need and hunger shining in them. The room could be on fire, and I wouldn't even notice. It wouldn't matter. Frozen and breathless, my legs can barely hold me straight as Sébastien takes deep breaths wrenched from his chest.

Drowning in emotion and guilt, I hold onto his shoulders for support. "I want it all," I say, breathing hard. "Everything with you. But I can't do that to my husband. Not while I'm still married to him." "I don't give a fuck about him." He takes my hand in his and places it on top of his heart. "Feel this? Does it feel wrong to you?" He grabs my head, pulling me closer to him, and kisses me hard. Breathlessly. "And what about this? Because ma petite chouette, it hasn't felt this fucking right to me in a very long time."

I shake my head, unable to utter a coherent thought. My conscience is at odds with my heart. I reach for his wrist, kissing his hand. "I can't. Please understand that."

"Why, Valentina? He isn't here with you. *I am.*"

"I know you are, you beautiful man." *But I can't begin something with you when* ... "I'm married. It would make me no better than him. And you deserve better."

I feel like I'm standing at a crossroads with one foot in the present and the other in the past. One road leads to William and the life we've built. The other leads to Sébastien and the unknown. I know which road I want to take, but I can't fully turn my back on the other until that path has been closed.

"Then what do you call what's been happening between us?"

"I don't know ... dreaming?"

"It hasn't been a fucking dream to me, Valentina. Not to me," he says, hurt in his eyes. "I'm falling for you for fuck's sake." He tries to take a step back. "I can't do this now."

"I'm so sorry." I let go of his wrist and wrap my arms around him as though trying to absorb him into me, desperation driving my every move. "I'll deal with this. I promise I'll make it right."

"I can't. Let go, Valentina." He shakes his head. His breathing spikes. "Because if I don't leave now, I'm going to kiss you again and I don't think I'll be able to stop this time, not until you're under me and my cock is buried deep inside you."

Sébastien pushes me away from him, leaving the apartment. The door slams and I remain standing there for a moment as I try to calm down. Lowering my gaze, I notice the battered state of my clothes. Shaking uncontrollably, I wrap my arms around me as tears leak out of my eyes. I wish I knew why I'm crying, but it's all a jumble in my head, in my heart. I cry because I am happy when I shouldn't be. I cry because I'm in love with a man who isn't my husband. And I cry because my husband doesn't deserve this kind of betrayal.

CHAPTER TWENTY

William

THE DAY STARTS LIKE any other. Nothing different. Nothing out of the ordinary. Wake up at five a.m. Go for a run. Come back at six fifteen. Take a shower. Get dressed in a gray suit, a perfectly starched white shirt, and red striped tie. It's all as it should be. Perfect. Precise. Monotonous. Calculated.

It's all a damn lie.

Deep down there's nothing but chaos because of my stupid, weak wife. She's almost cost me everything. But I've got a plan. A plan which will have her running back to me in no time.

Valentina's fatal flaw is that she cares too much, loves too much, and forgives too easily. She puts everyone before her and her own needs. If my coffee has grown cold, she prepares another pot so I can have fresh, hot coffee. If I'm having a shitty day, she's the first one to ask if there's anything she can do to make it better. I cheated on her and she stayed because she loved me too much. And if she's made to believe that I'm nothing without her, that I need her in my life to survive, she will come back to me with her tail between her legs for having hurt me.

It's that easy. That simple.

I skip the breakfast Evan, the chef, prepared for me and run out the door, getting in my car. On my way to Gwyneth's, I give Meredith a call and order her to cancel all my meetings for the day.

I arrive at Gwyneth's house, let myself in without ringing the doorbell, and go in search of my stepsister. She lives in one of those obnoxious mansions where flashy trumps elegance. She gets off on the knowledge that most people envy her beauty and wealth. The more people hate her, the happier she is. I've never understood it.

As I walk through a hall full of flashy paintings and statues, I run into one of the cleaning girls. Pretty, young thing. Upon seeing me, she blushes and drops the duster in her hand, stuttering an apology. I take in the rosy color of her cheeks, her dilated pupils, the catch in her breathing. She wants me, and if it weren't for the imperative need to talk to my sister, I might have given her sweet body a try. Bet she could fuck me real good.

Smiling my most charming smile, I ask her about Gwyneth.

She seems disoriented at first, blinking repeatedly. She clears her throat, takes a deep breath, and then tells me the whereabouts of my stepsister. She's still in her bedroom. Figures. Gwyneth subscribes to the belief that no one should be out of bed before eleven a.m.

"And her husband?" I ask, removing an imaginary piece of lint off my jacket.

"He just left, sir."

I pat the girl's cheek and tell her she's a good girl before sending her away. I watch her tight ass enclosed in the blue uniform my sister makes the help wear as she scurries away from me. *What a pity ...*

Without bothering to knock on her door first, I let myself in. Total darkness greets my eyes. A bored sigh escapes my lips as I cross the room, past the grand four-poster bed where Gwyneth is currently asleep, until I reach the windows. I pull back the blackout curtains letting the sun flood the four walls with its bright light. Satisfied, my gaze goes to Gwyneth, finding her lying on her stomach, the naked curves of her shoulder and back inviting.

I go to her, kneel at her bedside, and push aside the river of blond hair covering her face. Unable to have children, our parents adopted Gwyneth and I from different families when we were young. Raised in a foster care system that didn't care about me, I didn't know what love was until Marla adopted me. We grew up to love her as our own flesh and blood. When we were little, she used to call us her golden angels, saying that God had sent us to

116

LOVE ME IN THE DARK

watch over her and to fill her life with beauty. Father used to beat us because he couldn't stand looking at us.

"My sleeping beauty," I whisper laughingly in her ear, stirring her awake. My voice sounds rough as sand paper. "Shall I kiss you to see if you can be awoken?"

Gwyneth blinks the sleep away, her eyes getting used to me. "William."

My name coming from her sounds like a shared secret, an invitation. My mouth lands on her tender lips ever so gently, stealing the air she breathes. Sweetness and warmth, that's what this kiss tastes like. It's a friendly peck, but my body immediately reacts as a sense of coming home washes through me.

"Good morning," I say when the kiss comes to an end.

"What are you doing here?" she asks breathlessly, pressing her fingers on her lips as though she was trying to hold onto the sensation of my mouth on hers a bit longer. "Come to join me for a morning cuddle?"

I let go of her, straightening, and move to sit on the brocade chair next to the bed. Focusing on the midnight blue silk under my hands, I say, "I need you to do something for me, sis." I raise my eyes, scanning her face. "It has to do with Valentina."

Lifting herself on her elbows, the sheet barely covers her tits. She's aware that I can see she's naked under that flimsy piece of material, but she doesn't care. Like I said, my sister hasn't one modest bone in her.

"What did that piece of trash do now?" Her green eyes spark with dislike.

"Gwyneth ..." I warn her. "Remember you're talking about my wife."

She huffs. "Why do you care what I say about her? You don't even love her."

"You're right, I don't. But I find it distasteful when you speak about her in that manner. It bores me."

"Fine," she says, sounding like a petulant child who didn't get her way. "But why would you need my help? I'm the last person who could help you with her. Valentina hates my guts."

"It's Loretta." I cross my ankle over my knee and look out the window, finding her landscaping team already hard at work. I sigh, loathing being bothered this early in the morning. "She paid me a visit the other day. Somehow she found out that Valentina is in

Paris, and that she won't come back. She's gotten it into her head that if Valentina divorces me, she'll disinherit me," I drawl.

"What? Valentina isn't at your beck and call?" She chuckles, ignoring the part about our grandmother. "Well, that's news. Could it be possible that my big brother is losing his touch with women?"

In one swift movement, I'm straddling her lap as I run my hands over her fleshy tits covered in the sheet, flicking, pinching her already hard nipples and punishing her with my touch as I tear moans out of her body. I dip my head close to her ear and mouth her neck, savoring the taste of her sweat. "I don't even need to bury my fingers in your cunt right now to know you're wet." I bite her lip hard, making her cry out in pain. "I can smell it."

"You bastard." She grinds her pussy against my cock. She's needy as fuck and at my mercy. Just how I like them. "What do you want me to do?" She swallows, breathing heavily.

"I want you to go to Paris and bring her back. Tell her that I'm falling apart without her. Make her believe it."

"How am I supposed to do that?"

"Figure it out. I'm sure your pretty, little head can come up with something."

"Why don't you go?"

"Because she doesn't want to see me. She's also supposed to think I'm giving her the space she's asked for."

She chuckles. "You don't know women at all, do you?"

"What do you mean?"

She sighs. "*You* have to go get her, silly man. *Show* that *you* care. You know she's weak for you. You're her kryptonite. Work your magic, make the pathetic grand gesture, and she'll believe you." Gwyneth smirks, her eyes taunting me. "Besides, if she hasn't come back, maybe it's because there's someone else ..."

"That's impossible." I get off of her and the bed, my hands already missing the warmth of her skin. "But I see your point," I say as I walk to the door.

"Leaving already?" I hear her ask, her voice tinged with disappointment coming from behind.

I lock the door, making sure that no one will bother us. Then I turn around to look at her as a smile crosses my lips. A silent understanding passes between us, one that speaks of a bond that can't be explained or reasoned.

"What are you doing?" Gwyneth asks as she sits up, reclining her back against the bedframe. The silk sheet slips down her body like a waterfall. My cock stirs at the sight of her perfect tits, full and heavy, and so unlike my flat-chested wife.

"Think I'll keep you company for a while." I begin to tug at my tie, loosen it, as my feet move, closing the space between us. Lust makes my blood pump hard and fast.

"Oh yes?" She smiles hungrily like a cat about to feast on the poor unsuspecting canary. Pushing the sheet to the side, Gwyneth spreads her legs open for me without shame. "Want to join me after all?"

When I'm standing next to her, I lean down, reach out and twist her hair in my hand, tug her head back, and make her look at me. I absorb the fear, need, and want in her eyes, the sick bastard inside me feeding off of it, before I kiss my stepsister hard on the lips. It's a bruising, punishing, filthy kiss. Just how we like it.

As the kiss comes to an end, Gwyneth whispers against my lips, "No one kisses me like you do."

"Correction." I slowly unbuckle my belt, taking in the rosy color of her cheeks and her swollen lips. "No one fucks you like I do, little sister."

CHAPTER TWENTY-ONE

Valentina

IT'S BEEN TWO DAYS since I last saw Sébastien, and not a minute has gone by when he doesn't intrude my thoughts. When I don't yearn for him. Every atom of my body begs me to go to him, but I'm giving him the space he needs while I figure out what my next step is.

After he left me that night, alone in bed, I realized the idyll was over. And as much as it tore me apart, I knew it was time to wake up and fix my mess. I wasn't being fair to Sébastien and William. They both deserved better from me. But doubt was always one step behind me. Lurking. Whispering seductively in my ear. It made me question every choice and decision that had brought me to this point, coloring my future with uncertainty and fear. I hated it. I wanted to cover my ears while drowning out all the noise. But it wasn't working. I could hear everything. Loud and clear.

Could I throw it all away for a few wonderful months with Sébastien? What-ifs turned into more what-ifs, driving me mad.

There's a knock at the door, and I open it to find Sébastien standing in front of me. It takes all of my power to remain in place and not go to him. Throw myself at his feet. Beg him to take me. Before Sébastien came into my world, I thought life was as good as it was going to get. But then I was gifted a brief glimpse into a life where happiness wasn't something I had once known and forgotten all about. It became real. Tangible. It had the texture of a man. The intoxicating smell of his cologne. It sounded like his laughter. Felt like his arms around me. He showed me what it was to be happy, so ridiculously happy. However, as I stare at his achingly beautiful features, fear that this might be all gone corrodes me from the inside out.

And that's when I know the answer to all of my questions.

He walks in without saying a word. I can feel my pulse, hear it beating out of my chest as I shut the door behind me and turn to look at him, hoping to find the same answer in his eyes.

"Hi."

He comes to me until our bodies collide. Crash. The outline of his hard body molds against every soft curve of mine. The tips of my nipples tingle with desire. My core throbs for him. He wraps an arm around my waist as he splays the fingers of his other hand behind my head, pulling me closer to him.

"I want you to need me like I need you. Violate you like you violate my thoughts. Fill you without shame and mercy. Lose myself in your body and never come back," he hisses before crushing me in an embrace so hard, I feel the air escape my lungs. He quiets all the voices with this kiss. It's desperate. Needy. And then because we have nothing else left to lose, we jump over the abyss and fall.

What a beautiful death it is.

Sébastien ends the kiss first. "I'm sorry about the other night." He leans forward with his forehead pressed against mine as his hands go to the back of my neck, holding me captive with his blue gaze. "I lost my head. I thought that—have I lost you?"

I grip his tee with shaky hands, suddenly feeling like crying from joy. I can't continue to lie to myself. I'm aware it might be too soon but love knows no time. No rules. No boundaries. No logic. Love sees and recognizes its missing piece. And I'm staring at mine. "Late at night when I'm all alone, I replay you, Sébastien. I replay the beginning. The middle. The moment I knew. You don't have to make me choose because I choose you." I stand on my tiptoes to cover his face with frantic kisses as a tremor runs through him. Or maybe it's me. "I choose you."

"You asked me the other day if I felt this." I take his hand and place it over my heart. "Feel mine as it beats for you. Over and over. Again and again. Now. Tomorrow. Forever."

"Jesus Christ, Valentina. Come here," he adds before kissing me breathlessly, irrationally, and recklessly.

When we come up for air, I wrap my arms around his torso and tilt my head back to watch him as he towers over me. I smile.

A soft smile crosses his lips. "What?"

"I really, really like kissing you."

"Good." He grins. "Because I plan to kiss you for a very fucking long time."

Sobering up, I lean my cheek on him, the cotton of his shirt soft under my skin. "I'll call William tonight after I come back from Mr. Lemaire's."

"This is what you want?" Sébastien asks, placing a kiss on top of my head.

"It's just …" I bite my lip as I weigh my words carefully, but choose to be honest with Sébastien. I'm done with lies and hiding things. I want everything to be out in the open. For a moment, I wait for the guilt and the disgust I should be feeling to come, but they never do. "It's just it would be better to end things with William face to face. I should go and see him, but this will have to do for now. I don't want more lies."

"Want me to take you to the States?"

I shake my head, smiling softly. "Thank you, but I need to do this on my own."

"Fair enough." He runs his hands along my back, his warmth giving me strength. "It will all work out. You'll see."

"Promise?"

"Of course, ma petite chouette."

CHAPTER TWENTY-TWO

Valentina

THAT NIGHT AFTER WORK, I wait for the elevator to get to my floor, thoughts of seeing Sébastien already filling my head. My hands automatically go to my lips still full of him and smile. The warmth of his touch, of his embrace, of his kisses, still saturates my senses, enslaving me to their memory.

Still smiling, I get out of the elevator and freeze when my eyes land on the man sitting on the floor outside my apartment. His shoulders hunched remind me of a defeated man. His usually perfect blond hair is a mess. I feel like a bucket of cold water has been poured down on me.

He looks up, his gaze flooded with pain. "Hello Valentina," my husband says sadly, standing up. "Can we talk?"

CHAPTER
TWENTY-THREE
Valentina

I NOD, OPENING THE door to my apartment. For a moment, I think my eyes are betraying me as I watch William walk in. Because even though I *know* the man standing in front of me is my husband, he doesn't *look* like him. This man seems hollow. Empty. His usual radiance is gone and has been replaced by sorrow.

"What are you doing here?" I close my eyes, the floor beneath my feet suddenly shaky. "I mean, what are you doing in Paris?"

"I wanted to see you. I miss you." He buries his hands in his jeans, staring at the floor. "How are you?"

"Good ... you?" I ask tentatively.

"I don't know ..." He tears his gaze away from the floor and looks me in the eye. "Nothing's the same since you left."

I suck in my breath, his words like bullets. "I don't know what you want me to say, William." Suddenly the room spins around me. I grip the table in the foyer for support. "Truth be told, I don't even know what to think about you being here after all this time without a phone call or a text message."

"I'm not the only guilty one here, Valentina. You stopped calling, too."

His simple accusation slaps me across the face. It stings and hurts. The truth behind it leaves a mark in the red-hot color spreading on my cheeks.

"I'm sorry, darling. There was no need for that."

"No, I deserved that," I say, crossing my arms to stop them from shaking. My gaze lands briefly on my wedding ring, and I remember the vows I made to William. Vows I've broken since the moment I arrived here. William's presence is like a hammer, beating me down over and over again. I hang my head in shame and study the carpeted floor.

"Would you like to sit?"

"I'm good."

"Okay." Needing a distraction, I go to the kitchen and pour myself a glass of wine. "Drink?"

"No, thank you."

He joins me in the kitchen, and his nearness sends my heartbeat into overdrive. When he's standing next to me, he pulls me into his arms and holds me in a tight embrace.

"Please don't." I try to push him away, unable to look at him. My insides are torn to shreds. *This is my husband,* I tell myself. His embrace should be welcome, but it isn't. Not anymore.

"Let me hold you if only for this moment," he says, his voice heavy with emotion. "I'm so sorry, my darling." He places a fingertip under my chin, making me look at him, his eyes pleading and full of sorrow.

"William ..." *Tell him about Sébastien. Tell him it's over.* "I ... we need to—"

"Please come back home."

"I don't know if I can, William. So much has happened."

"I know it has, but your life is back in Greenwich. With me. I need you. Don't you see? You're what keeps me together ..." He strokes my cheek with the back of his hand. "Before you, I thought I was lost."

"I didn't trust love. Didn't trust people. I was an island—an island that no one could reach. But one day, it all changed. I learned to trust. I learned to trust love, and it was because of you. I love you, Val. And without you ..." He lets go of me, his hands falling down to his sides as though in surrender. "I don't know what will become of me. Maybe my father was right about me ..."

"I don't understand. What about your father?" Every time I've tried to broach the subject of his childhood after reminiscing about my own, it's like hitting a wall. He either changes the subject or quiets me with kisses, making me forget. Eventually, I learned to respect his silence hoping that one day he'd feel comfortable enough to share that part of himself with me.

"I know I never talk about him." He pauses, measuring his next words carefully. "There's a reason for that." He chuckles wryly. "Let's just say he was never going to win an award for Father of the Year."

I knit my brows in confusion, an ominous feeling settling in the pit of my stomach. "What do you mean?"

"You've seen the scar on my back."

I nod, preparing myself for what he's about to say.

"Do you remember what I told you about it?"

"You told me your German shepherd got loose and bit your back. He took out a chunk of your skin. You ended up in the hospital for days because the wound got infected."

"Max didn't get loose by accident," he says quietly, his face devoid of emotion. "I tried protecting my mother and Gwyneth from him, but it only incensed him more. The beatings got nastier, more frequent. I was really happy when he died. I hated him."

Sorrow for them makes the strings of my heart twist and knot until they are impossible to untie.

"I drowned in hate. It festered in my blood. Something inside me changed forever. He used to say I was unworthy of being loved, and I believed him. I wore his words and hate like armor. That is until you."

"Oh, William." I wrap my arms around him, pulling him close to me, my heart breaking for him and the boy he used to be.

"I need you, Val. You're the glue that keeps me together." He returns my embrace, desperation vibrating in his hold. "I haven't been able to think, eat, or sleep. I keep punishing myself for destroying our marriage. The one good thing in my life."

Maybe I've gotten it all wrong. I've painted him as the villain in my story, but maybe it's been me all along.

That's when all the guilt comes crashing down on me. God. What have I done? I'm swallowed by it. Drowned by it. I've held his affair like a gun to William's head for over a year now. And what have I been doing in the meantime? Losing my head over another man.

"I was a fucking fool to not cancel everything and come to Paris straight away. Am I too late? You keep giving me chances, and I keep fucking up, but this is the last time. If you take me back, it won't ever happen again. It's been hell without you." He kisses my forehead. "I cannot lose you ... I can't," he utters passionately. "Please forgive me, my darling."

With each sentence he utters, a chasm grows between Sébastien and me. He drifts further and further away from me as reality settles around me.

My gaze roams over William's dear face as memories of our lifetime together surround me, drawing me back to him. And I remember the dream—the dream we had together. The life we made flashes before my eyes. Twelve years worth. Did I really think I could walk away from him just like that?

"You know what the real wonders of life are?" I asked William as I sat astride his lap. He cupped my bare ass in his large hands and pushed me flush against his erection.

"Yes." He leaned down, nuzzling my neck. "One of them is fucking my wife."

I groaned, his kisses raising and tickling my skin, lighting me up like a grenade. "Do be serious."

William chuckled and raised his head, his eyes locked with mine. Seconds passed in silence. He grew serious—thoughtful—his easy, teasing smile gone. "I don't care for buildings and statues. They're just things. You are my real wonder, Val. Waking up next to you and making love to you." He rubbed his cheek against mine. "You're everything that makes me good and worthy."

A bomb full of memories hits me in the middle of the chest. It pierces through me and spills all the shame flowing in my veins. "We can't go on as we are. Things need to change, William."

"I know, my darling. Things will, you'll see." He showers my face with kisses. "Without you I am nothing, you hear? Nothing. I love you so damn much, Val."

"I love you, too," I say, but the words taste like acid on my tongue. He leans down, his mouth searching for mine, but I can't. At the last second, I turn my face to the side and his kiss lands on my cheek.

"Everything will be all right now," he says. "I'll prove it to you."

His words should be a soothing balm, but instead, they close about me like a jail.

"Let's leave Paris."

"What?" I blink as though waking up from a dream. "Now?"

"Yes, there's nothing keeping us here. Let's go home, Val," he pleads tenderly.

But there is. There is!

I nod, a knot in the pit of my stomach, suddenly feeling like I'm going to be sick. "Okay."

"I flew in the jet. I'm sure it can be ready in an hour. Do you need more time?"

I shake my head numbly. "I don't need that long."

"Do you still employ that driver?"

"Pierre? Yes. Would you like me to call him?"

"No need. Give me his number and I'll set everything up."

"Sure."

In the bedroom, I toss all my things in the suitcases, a storm of clothes, bags, and shoes swirling around me. I finish packing in no time. Ready to close the door behind me, my gaze lands on the wooden owl sitting on the nightstand. I give into weakness and allow myself to think of the man expecting me tonight.

And it hurts. It hurts so much.

I want to cry, but the tears won't come—I don't deserve them. These are the consequences of my actions—the big fucking reality of it all. Karma has finally found me, and she is merciless in her punishment. But I knew she would eventually catch up to me and demand her payment.

Unable to look at the owl anymore, I shut the door, hearing it click behind me—the sound final—unforgiving. I take a few steps toward the living room where William and Pierre are waiting for me, but change my mind halfway there. *I can't. I can't. I can't.* Spinning on my feet, I go back inside for the wooden figure, the only thing I have left of a beautiful dream, now just a memory.

As I step outside, Sébastien's gift in my bag, I come to the realization that pushing him out of my heart would be like asking the sun to stop rising every morning—an impossibility. He's dug himself so deep in my skin, in the marrow of my bones, that if you were to cut me open, you'd find parts of me, William, and Sébastien intertwined. But I can do one thing for my husband, and that is to never look back, putting Sébastien out of my mind. My heart screams that it's impossible, and every part of my soul cries. However, I turn a deaf ear to it all.

I will do it for William.

"Ready?" he asks, rising from the couch.

Hollow, I nod. We make our way to the entrance. Pierre opens it for us, and we step out of the apartment. I hear him shut the door behind us, the sound like an arrow through the chest. I take one step.

Two steps.

Three steps.

"Wait. I can't. I can't."

William glances back, confusion embedded in his features. "Excuse me?"

"I …" I turn on my feet. "I have to say goodbye."

He frowns. "To whom?"

I shake my head, leaving him without an explanation. Desperation and urgency propel me to move faster. I take the stairs, climb two at a time until I get to his floor. I can't even think what I'm going to say to him. All I know is that I need to see him one last time. Maybe try to explain.

I raise a hand and knock and knock, but there's no answer.

Come on, Sébastien. Open the damn door.

I knock again and ring the doorbell. *Come on.* Again. *Come on.* Again. *Come on.* Again.

Slowly, little by little, the light goes out until there's nothing left but darkness. Funny that, how hearts can continue to beat when they feel as though they are breaking into a thousand pieces.

I wait a minute, and another, and another. But Sébastien never comes to the door, and no magic ping of the elevator brings him to me.

My eyes blur as tears begin to fall down my cheeks and a sob is torn from my chest. I place my palm on the cool wood, leaning my head against it. "Maybe in another life we'll meet again and get it right. But whatever happens, you will always remain my one perfect memory, my one perfect dream. I love you, my beautiful man."

I take a moment to collect myself, wipe my tears, and go back downstairs.

William puts his cellphone away in the back pocket of his jeans when he notices me. He clears his throat. "Everything okay?"

"Sorry about that." My gaze lands briefly on Pierre, and the sadness and understanding I see in his eyes almost undoes me. It takes every ounce of willpower I own not to fall apart. "I wanted to say goodbye to a neighbor who's …" I suck in a breath, "who's helped me a lot."

"Who is it?" His frown grows deeper. "Maybe I should thank him too."

"No, that's okay. It's the same lady I mentioned a while back. The one who invited me to her dinner party," I lie, feeling like I'm going to be sick.

William seems to take my word for it, and I breathe a sigh of relief. "I'll have my assistant send her an arrangement of flowers when we get home." He takes my hand in his, and we start to move toward the elevator, leaving the apartment behind.

I'm staring out the window, watching cars become blurs of colors, when I remember Sébastien's painting. Desperation makes me want to go back for it, but it's too late. Leaning forward to speak to Pierre, I ask him if he can go back to the apartment tomorrow, retrieve the painting for me, and have it shipped to Greenwich.

"Of course."

"Thank you so much," I say, feeling an explosion of gratitude toward Pierre. "Don't worry about the cost. I'll transfer whatever you need to your account."

He nods, stopping at a red light.

Then, I remember Mr. Lemaire and more guilt corrodes me.

I look at William sitting to my left. He's on the phone with the pilot of the jet going over the details of our flight.

"Pierre, I have one last favor to ask from you," I say quietly, leaning forward.

"Oui, madame."

"Could you stop by Mr. Lemaire's and explain to him that I had to go home and that I'm so sorry."

Pierre nods, and I give him the address of the store. "Will you not be coming back to Paris?" he asks, our eyes connecting in the rearview mirror.

Deflated. Empty. Numb.

I shake my head. "No, Pierre. I don't think I am."

CHAPTER TWENTY-FOUR

WHEN THE WHEELS OF the jet touch down on the runway of Westchester County Airport, the sun has been out for a couple of hours. I lean my head back on the leather seat and close my eyes, emotionally battered as though I had just come out of a war zone. But it's a new day, a new beginning—a new chance to start all over again. So I pick myself up and keep going, bruises and all, Sébastien and my time in Paris locked in a corner deep in the recesses of my mind.

As the jet taxies to the terminal, I focus on the wet asphalt covered in puddles that shine with oil rainbows. The plane comes to a stop on the tarmac, and the cheery voice of the pilot announcing our arrival awakens me from my trance.

William kisses my forehead. "We're home, my darling."

I nod, swallowing the lump in my throat and forcing myself to look him in the eye. "Yes, we are."

Our home seems to have been untouched in the time I was gone. The same paintings hang on the wall. The same large columns fill the hallway leading to the grand staircase. The familiar smells of lemon and wood saturate my nose. Everything is as it should be yet nothing is the same.

William helps me out of my coat while I scan the foyer. It feels like a lifetime ago since I was last here. When his fingers brush the back of my neck, a shiver runs down my spine. I swallow, closing my eyes momentarily.

Away from Paris, reality is becoming harder to ignore. Every move made, word spoken becomes tentative. Careful. Measured. They say, *Please, let me back in. Remember this—remember us. We used to love each other. We still do. You hurt me. I hurt you. I'm sorry. I'm sorry, too. Don't give up on us.*

"Val," he whispers, tenderly wrapping his fingers around my upper arms from behind as he steps closer to me.

I suck in a ragged breath as the heat of his hands settles in my bones. Somewhere deep inside me, there's a home built on our lives together, its walls made out of memories, love, dreams, pain, beauty, and suffering. I thought its doors were shut, but I hear him now, knocking, begging me to let him inside.

I hesitate, and William knows it.

Gently, he spins me around until we're facing each other. I study his features. He's William, my husband. But my treacherous heart remains quiet.

He lets go of my arms to cup my face softly between his palms. I cover his hands with mine.

"This time apart …" William leans down and kisses the crests of my cheeks, my eyebrows, my mouth. Each time his lips come into contact with me, the door rattles, shaking the foundation of the house. "I thought I lost you for good. I couldn't breathe. My life—" His voice breaks as his touch grows more possessive, more desperate. "My life has no meaning without you."

And then I ask the one question I told myself I wouldn't because it might open the Pandora's box, but I need to know. I need to hear it from him. "Why did you wait so long to come to Paris?"

William takes a breath as hesitation flashes across his eyes. "I thought about it, but then you asked for space. For time. And after all the shit I've put you through, I thought the least I could do was to respect your wishes. It wasn't smart of me, but I didn't know what else to do." He takes my hand in his. "It hurt like hell, Val. But it taught me a very valuable lesson."

His pull grows stronger. As I stare at the naked pain in his gaze, I want to self-flagellate, draw my own blood. I put it there. The guilt for what I've done to him becomes a cross I carry on my shoulders, pulling me down.

"It took me almost losing you to realize how much I need you. How much I love you." He raises my hand to his lips, kissing it.

"Some days I told myself to go anyway, to beg you to come back. Fuck the space you asked for. But I was afraid of what I would find."

"What was that?"

"You. Making a life without me. I know you had every right, but it would've killed me. To know and *see* that you didn't need me to be happy. And the thought of you moving on ..." He closes his eyes briefly. "I waited day in and day out until I couldn't anymore. I had to see you."

I drown in remorse for that's exactly what I was doing. Back in Paris, inebriated by Sébastien and the alluring unknown, it was easier to think that I could walk away from William. Gone was the mundane. The painful reminders. The memories. Suddenly, life was beautiful again. Everything was new. Exciting. Bright. And easy, so easy.

But away from all of it, I realize how naïve I was. Love is only part of what makes a marriage work. Marriage isn't about keeping tabs on who's fucked up the most. It's about taking those mistakes and working through them. Marriage is about commitment and forgiving—truly forgiving—and not giving up.

Is it stupid to let him back in once again? I don't know. But I can't throw this away because of a beautiful dream. *Sébastien was more than that,* my heart yells, but I ignore it. I tuck that love in a place that William will never be able to reach, a place that belongs to Sébastien and Sébastien alone; a place between heaven and hell, torment and delight. I focus on William who anchors me to the present, to the now, to this life. Underneath all the hurt and disappointment, he's still my husband and the man I fell in love with a long time ago. Besides, who am I to judge him? My hands are just as dirty as his. My aunt used to say that those who live in glass houses shouldn't throw stones. Therefore I take my dirty stones and put them back in my pocket. I capitulate. I open the door and let him back in.

I cup William's jaw and make him look at me as I say goodbye to my sun and beautiful dream. "It's all in the past."

"I will make this right, I promise," he says earnestly before kissing me, and this time I don't turn my face away. He erases the memory of another man's kiss and replaces it with his. My heart shouts that this is wrong, that these aren't the arms, the lips I want, but I ignore that voice and its pleas as I try to lose myself in the taste of his mouth. And when he reaches for me, taking my clothes off, touching every part of my body, I let him.

He spreads my legs and settles between them, entering me in one swift thrust. I let him fill me over and over again, come inside me, claim me until I can't feel or think anymore, and I'm swallowed by darkness. Welcome it.

There's no more music. No more laughter.

I do anything to make the pain and memories go away until there's nothing but numbness. But it doesn't work.

Every part of my soul cries for another man.

Oh, Sébastien ...

PART TWO

CHAPTER
TWENTY-FIVE
Valentina

NIGHT HAS FALLEN, but the wedding reception is just getting started.

The rich scent of roses drifts in the air, and the band's playing a Tony Bennett oldie, the male singer crooning charmingly for the audience. The expansive lawn of the country club has been turned into a magical forest lit by twinkling lights. Part of me says, *enjoy, Valentina!* But I can't bring myself to feel anything. Not one damn thing.

As I look around me, surrounded by so many people, so much exuberance, I have never felt more alone. There are times when I feel like a small fish in a vast sea, swimming against the direction of the current, unable to break free from it. And the more I fight the current, the harder it is to swim. I'm drowning, and I can do nothing but smile.

I take a sip of wine and watch the bride as she slow dances with her handsome husband, one of William's cronies from grad school. He leans forward to whisper something in her ear while his pinky finger caresses her shoulder, and she throws her head back, laughing. It's the perfect shot. I hope the photographer caught it. I hope they remain that happy for as long as they can …

"Hey, you," a woman says, bumping my shoulder with hers.

I turn to look at my friend and smile naturally for the first time in what feels like a long time. "Gigi, hi."

We kiss on the cheeks and stare at each other. "Couldn't miss the wedding of the year," she adds saucily.

I chuckle. "Like you would care."

Her gaze lands on the bride and groom, her features softening. "Actually, I love weddings. Always have." She shrugs, raising her glass to her lips and gulping some of the white wine down. "Anyway, I'd heard you were back," Gigi says, focusing on me once again.

"Yep," I say, popping the sound of the p. "Paris was nice, but it was time to come home."

She raises a perfect eyebrow. "Are you sure about that?"

"I'm not sure what you mean." *But I know. I know.*

"What about, oh I don't know…" She traces a crack on the balustrade. "A certain gorgeous French man?"

And there it is again, the pain. The kind that no amount of alcohol will soothe or make you forget. I hide it behind smiles I don't feel, but my heart knows. It remembers every single day. And no matter how long it's been, there are times when it hurts so much I can hardly breathe.

"We were just friends," I say softly.

She scoffs in an unladylike manner. "Friends don't look at each other that way, Val."

"Please, Gigi. I'd rather not talk about it." Suddenly cold, I fold my arms across my chest and look at the ground, dispassionately noticing green and brown stains from the grass on the bottom of my gown. "It's all in the past."

"Is it?" Gigi asks wisely.

Ever since I came back a month ago, I've thrown myself into my old life while trying to make a new one with William. Days have turned into more days and more days, and William has been true to his word. Gone are the long hours at work. The lonely nights. He showers me with love and affection every chance he gets. He's also accepted to go to marriage therapy with me. But late at night, when my guard is down, it's hard not to admit that it's all a fraud.

I'm a fraud.

Sébastien is everywhere. In rainstorms. The taste of wine. I close my eyes, and he's there waiting for me to come back to him. Lost in agony, I wish, beg, for one more glimpse of him. But I continue to hold onto this pain because it's all I have left of

Sébastien, and I would rather live in hell for the rest of my days than to let him go. It's his memory alone that sustains me, giving me the strength to keep going in the empty vastness that is life without him.

I place my hands on the stone balustrade, still warm from being exposed to the sun all day. Raising my eyes to the sky, I try to admire the dark blanket twinkling with embedded stars. It reminds me of another evening similar to this when the night was young and a hypnotizing man invited me to dance. In that single, eternal moment life was full of magic, beautiful possibilities.

I chuckle when I really feel like crying. Bring a hand to my chest almost expecting to find a gaping hole there. I ripped my own heart out when I left him, and now there is nothing there. Nothing. Sometimes doing the right thing breaks you the most.

"You know why people lie, Gigi?"

"It's easier than facing the truth?"

I bite my lip, a rock lodged in the back of my throat. "Because sometimes the truth hurts more than a lie ever could."

She reaches for my hand. "Val—"

"There you are," I hear my husband say before he wraps an arm around my waist, his heat seeping in my bones. He places a soft kiss on the curve of my neck. "I've been looking for you, my darling."

I give my head a tiny shake as I try to compose myself, pasting a smile for William. "Hey ... I've been here catching up with Gigi."

For a few tense seconds he studies me as though he knows I'm full of shit before addressing her. "Gigi, how do you do? Long time no see."

"William," Gigi says, watching him with open dislike. She's one of the few who isn't dazzled by William and his perfect looks.

"I'm going to have to steal my wife for a moment." He smiles at her and then focuses on me. "There's someone I want you to meet." He grips my arm, starting to guide me toward the bar. "Gigi. Great seeing you as always."

"Let's catch up soon, all right?" I throw the words in the air at her before following William.

"Sure, you have my number."

I glance over my shoulder to find her gazing at us, a frown lodged between her eyebrows as she raises her hand and waves goodbye.

"Are you all right, my darling?" I hear William ask, drawing my attention back to him. He's so close I can feel the heat of his body warming me. "You seemed upset just now."

"It's nothing really, just a little under the weather."

William pauses mid-step, turning toward me. Cupping the side of my face, his thumb rubs the crest of my cheek. "Would you like to go home?"

The concern in his voice unravels me. *This is why I stay.* Without giving my actions another thought, I turn my lips toward his palm and kiss it. "No, it's okay. I'll be fine."

"That's my Val." He smiles his most charming smile. "Come. I see my friends that I want you to meet."

We join a small group of people. I recognize some, and William introduces me to those whom I don't. He makes a joke. Tells an anecdote. It doesn't matter. All eyes are on him. Eating out of the palm of his hand. You can see the women falling in love with him, and the men secretly hating him while wanting to be him.

I take in the line of his aristocratic nose, the curve of his full lips, his razor-sharp jaw and sculpted cleft chin. He's mesmerizing. Larger than life. He runs his fingers through his longish blond locks, and memories of his hair blowing wildly in the wind the day we drove to meet his grandmother, both of us living life out loud, momentarily hold me captive. I should be happy. Elated that he's mine. But as I stare at my husband laughing bombastically at some kind of joke, I have to keep telling myself—reminding myself— that this is what I want.

I repeat those words over and over again until I carve them on my bloody skin.

Maybe then, I'll finally believe them.

CHAPTER TWENTY-SIX

Sébastien

THE HOTEL BAR IS EMPTY. Just the bartender and me. She asks if I want another one as she wipes the counter with a tablecloth, and I raise my half-empty beer bottle.

"I'm good."

But am I? I don't even fucking know anymore.

I'm split in two. Agony and anger. I go from missing Valentina with an ache in my soul to wanting to erase her from my heart, from my head, cursing her for leaving me. I tell myself that I'll forget her, but even those words sound empty to my ears. Her memory is my tormentor and savior.

My hell and paradise.

I focus my attention on the bottle in my hands before bringing it to my lips and taking a swig. My life was empty before her, but I was content. Satisfied. And now? My body is here. It appears whole. But there's nothing inside. She took it all with her when she left.

The air in my lungs...

The beating of my heart...

There is only silence now where there was laughter before. Only darkness where there was once blinding hope. She showed me how beautiful life could be again, but she didn't fucking teach

141

me how to live without her, how to breathe without her. So I welcome the numbness, seeking—waiting for the abyss to swallow me whole. I've been there before, after all.

The bottle empty, I ask the bartender for one more. I drink to forget, but the more I drink, the more I remember her. The more it hurts.

Oh, Valentina ... why did you have to fucking leave me, too?

As she places a new one in front of me and takes away the empty bottle, I stare at her. She's a brunette with a friendly smile. *Pretty.* "Merci."

"De rien." When our gazes connect, she says, "A horse walks into a bar. The bartender asks, 'why the long face?'"

"Good one," I say without laughing.

She shrugs. "Thought you needed a good laugh, but I don't think it worked."

"What makes you say that?"

"You've been scowling at the poor bottles in your hand this past hour, *and* you're still scowling. No wonder my bar is empty," she teases again.

"Have I been here for that long?" I ask dispassionately, noticing the tattoo of an orchid vine crawling up her arm for the first time. The image is like a visceral stab to the gut, slicing me fucking open.

"Longer." She frowns. "Everything all right?"

Shaking my head, I pretend to smile when every part of me howls in pain. "Everything's fine."

"All right," she says, doubt embedded in her gaze. "Give me a shout if you need anything else."

Another customer arrives at that moment sitting on the other side of the bar. She goes to him to take his order, and as I watch her walk away from me, a sudden yearning for her company comes over me. Maybe talking to her will silence the taunting ghost of Valentina, and offer me a brief respite from the hell I'm drowning in.

When she makes her way back to my side, she smiles politely before going back to polishing glasses meticulously.

"Can I ask you something?" I ask, peeling off the label of the beer to keep my hands busy.

"Fire away."

I focus on the colorful array of bottles behind her, tracing back my steps that day, searching for the moment when everything went wrong.

I left Valentina standing outside her apartment, my soul and body at her feet. She had to go to work, and I had to deliver some paintings. We made plans to see each other later that night. On my way back from the gallery, I got a call from a frantic Sophie. Her babysitter had cancelled last minute, and she needed my help to watch the kids while she went to an appointment. I told her not to worry, never imagining that by the time I made it back to the apartment, Valentina would be gone.

I went looking for her. After knocking for about five minutes, I gave up, sat outside her door, and waited. I knew she would eventually come. Maybe she got stuck late at work. Sophie had mentioned she'd seen her earlier in the day and had placed a large order of arrangements. Maybe that was it. But after an hour turned into two, a bad feeling sunk its teeth around me, and no amount of excuses would shake it off. I told myself to calm down. To not worry. There was an explanation why Valentina wasn't here yet. Before I drove myself crazy, I decided to go back to my place and wait for the next morning. I would go downstairs, and she'd be there. Everything would be all right again. It had to be.

But when I went downstairs the next morning, I didn't find Valentina. Instead, I found a real estate agent along with a cleaning crew erasing all traces of her. Hiding behind neighborly concern, I asked the agent what had happened to Valentina. The agent told me the apartment was being put on the market again. The woman who had lived there had gone back to the United States and wasn't planning on coming back.

I broke out into a cold sweat. She had left me without an explanation. Without even saying fucking goodbye.

And like a stupid, pathetic fuck, I waited for her to come back to me. Hours turned into days and days turned into weeks. Eventually I gave up, drank heavily, and took random women to bed. Fucking harder, fucking to oblivion.

I laugh bitterly. I tried so damn hard to do the right thing by Valentina, take it at her speed. I didn't even fuck her.

I lost her anyway.

What a fucking joke.

She was once my hope, but the love I felt for her became my prison. The spiral down was a brief relief. Yet late at night, with the smell of sex surrounding me and the taste of stale beer on my tongue, I couldn't fool myself anymore. It wasn't working. Nothing was. I still felt the pain. Raw. Unforgiving.

When Poppy and our unborn child died, I didn't think I could go on without them. Sorrow, anger, disbelief, they all drove me to madness. I purposefully threw myself in danger's way. If they couldn't be with me, I'd join them. One day, I sat there with a knife in my hand. I was fucking done. Tired. I couldn't handle the pain anymore. I kept thinking that it would be very easy to put an end to my pathetic, worthless life. But as I felt the sharp bite of the blade on my skin, I realized that I couldn't do it. Poppy wouldn't have wished for this. She would have wanted me to fight. Be the man she fell in love with.

I sought help the very same night.

Not everyone is lucky enough to get a second chance, and I did. I was gifted one in Valentina.

Or so I thought.

And no matter how low I sink in debauchery, I still can't let go of her.

There are times, though, like right now when I try to replay the whole sequence of events. Search for a sign that Valentina was lying to me. That what we shared had been nothing but wishful thinking. It would make it so damn easy to hate her. To move on. But deep in my heart, there's a voice screaming that what we had was real. That something happened to make her leave.

"Well?" the bartender asks, bringing me out of my reverie. "What was your question?"

Blinking repeatedly, I focus on her.

She grabs a bottle of whiskey, and pours a shot, handing me a small glass filled with liquid courage. "On the house. Now drink and then talk."

"Cheers." I down it, enjoying the burn as it is going down. "Thanks." I grin ruefully. "Guess I needed that."

She shrugs a tiny shoulder. "You pick up some tricks along the way working here. So, who is she?"

"Am I that obvious?"

She laughs. "No. Just a lucky guess."

I slide the shot glass back and forth between my hands, avoiding meeting her gaze as I consider what and how much to tell her. I'm not sure if it's the whiskey or her soothing presence, but I find myself opening up and unloading all of my bullshit. I tell her about Valentina and our time together, about the last morning I saw her, and how it seemed like it was finally going to work out only to come home and find her gone.

"That's my pathetic story." I grip my hair in my hands, wanting to pull it out. "It just doesn't make any sense that she left without even talking to me."

"Do you love her?"

I nod. "Fucking hopelessly." Even if William loved her for the rest of his life, it would only be a fraction of how much I love her in one beat of my worthless heart.

"There has to be a reason why she left." She removes the empty bottle and shot glass in front of me. I notice this time she doesn't ask me if I want another one. "Call me crazy, but there has to be more to her story. When you love someone, you just don't up and leave without a word. Husband or not. And by what you told me, I don't think it was an easy decision for her. There has to be a reason why she left the way she did. And if I were in your shoes, I would find out. I'd want closure."

"But what if—" I suck in a breath, an earthquake of emotion rolling through me. "I'm fucking afraid of what I'll find."

"We can't live our life in fear." She places a hand on my forearm, the touch welcoming—fortifying. "Imagine what you could lose because of it."

Her words bounce around me like a wrecking ball, little by little tearing down the walls I've erected since Valentina left. She's right. I've given enough of my life to fear, letting it rule over my every decision. And I'm done.

Done.

If there's a chance that Valentina returns my love, I will seize and fight for it.

And if …

No. I won't allow those doubts to haunt me.

I stare at the woman standing in front of me and thank God for sending her to me. He knew I needed her.

I take out a bill large enough to cover my drinks and then some, and place it on the table. She smiles, her eyes twinkling with pleasure.

"Had enough to drink?"

"Think so." I crack the first real smile I've felt in a very long time. "Thank you for everything."

"No problem."

I stand up, pushing the chair behind and heading toward the entrance. I'm almost past the threshold when I hear her ask, "What are you going to do now?"

I glance back. "Choose life."

Outside the hotel, the city comes alive, pulsating to the mad beating of my heart. I take out my phone and dial Sophie. She answers after the first ring.

"What's up, handsome?"

"Your best friend ... Her husband's family is from Greenwich, right?"

"Sharon? She's from New Canaan, her husband's from Texas. But, yeah, they live there now. Why do you ask?"

"Listen, I need you to do me a favor ..."

"Sure. Are you okay? You sound funny."

I stare at the cars flying by.

I choose life.

I choose her.

"Yeah," I pause. "I think I will be."

CHAPTER
TWENTY-SEVEN
Valentina

"GOOD MORNING, VAL."

I'm reaching for a pan in one of the cabinets when I see Evan approaching. He's been working as our chef for the past three years. He used to work at an Italian restaurant that we frequented in Port Chester until William made him an offer that he couldn't resist. Now he's with us.

"Good morning, Evan," I say lightly, placing the pan on the stove. "I'm preparing breakfast today." I open another cabinet and reach for a bowl this time.

He comes to stand next to me and folds his arms across his slim chest. He reminds me of a young George Clooney, back when he was on *E.R.* And unlike Mrs. Croft, who has never really warmed up to me, Evan has become a good friend. One of the few real friends I have.

"Should I be worried about my job?" he jokes, his dark eyes sparkling with humor.

I laugh. "Not at all. I woke up and felt like cooking."

He opens the glass container with the flour and hands it to me. "Pancakes?"

"Thank you, and yes."

"You're welcome." His gaze follows my every move, watching me scoop the flour and depositing it in the bowl. "Family recipe?"

"Yep, my aunt's. She used to wait tables at a diner back home." I grin, remembering the day she came home, a smug smile on her face because she finally got Johnny, the cook and owner of the diner, to share his famous recipe with her. "She got the recipe from the owner, who got it from his grandmother, and so forth. Would you like to try them?"

He rubs the back of his neck. "I'm not sure. I really should be making them for you."

I throw him a pointed look. "Evan, eat the damn pancakes."

Evan chuckles. "All right, boss."

I prepare a plate for him and place it in front of him. As I watch him reach for his knife and fork, I feel excited and nervous to find out what he thinks. He takes a bite and closes his eyes oohing and ahhing.

He swallows the first bite. "Fuck." He takes another bite. "These are something else."

"Pretty amazing, right?" I lean my hip on the counter as I watch him dig in, quite proud of myself. I reach for my coffee and take a sip, enjoying the taste of the Colombian brew. "Tell me, did you always know you wanted to be a chef?"

Evan takes the last bite, leaving his plate completely clean. Wipes his mouth with a napkin and turns his attention back to me. "No," he chuckles, "I went to dental school, but flunked out. Too much partying and drinking. I think my heart just wasn't in it, you know? My parents were pretty pissed, so they kicked me out and stopped paying my bills. They said it was time I got a dose of reality. It sucked really bad for a while."

"Because you had no money?"

"Well, that and because I had no idea what I wanted to do with my life. I was crashing at Lara's at the time. Every morning I woke up and watched her get ready for her internship, she was excited to go to work and learn. And there I was just sitting around, playing Xbox, waiting for my girlfriend to come home. Waiting for life to start."

"I like that … waiting for life to start."

"I felt useless, you know?"

If Evan only knew how much I understand. "I think I have an idea."

"Do you really?" he asks, surprise registering in the tone of his voice.

I nod, not wanting to elaborate. "So, what did you do?" I ask quietly, holding onto his next words as though they were the answer to my own questions.

"Well, I enjoyed cooking. Until then I'd considered it a hobby, something I was good at but never really thought about it as a career. But one day, Lara suggested I talk to her uncle who owned a diner in Bayside. Maybe he could give me a job. I drove all the way to Queens, and the rest is history." He stands up to place the plate in the sink. "Cooking is not only a job; it's my passion. What about you?"

"What about me?" I ask, playing dumb.

"Any passions?"

"Well, I enjoy cooking for sure." I put down the coffee mug on the counter and play with the handle. "But I wouldn't call it a passion necessarily." Memories of the lovely afternoons spent in Mr. Lemaire's flower shop tending to the flowers, making them come alive once again swirl around me. "Flowers," I say slowly, smiling. "Flowers are my passion." Their beauty, their smell, the way they brighten a room with color, bringing it to life. "They make me happy."

He pauses, seemingly measuring his next words. "You know, my sister owns a small flower shop in Rye. Nothing fancy, but she's happy. Busy. Would you like me to find out if she's looking for help?"

My heart begins to drum madly as my soul growls in hunger for the chance to taste this opportunity, to sink my teeth in, swallow it, and let it nourish me. Ever since I came back from Paris, there's a hunger in me that wasn't there before. I'm tired of sitting around and letting life pass me by. No, I want to be someone I am proud of. So the old Valentina and the new meet and collide like waves crashing against rocks. And I'm okay with it, because I know I will find my footing.

"Would you really do that for me?"

"Sure. Why not?"

I stare out the window, watching the morning sky, and get swept away by hope. Maybe things do have a way to work themselves out.

"What's the special occasion?"

Glancing over my shoulder, I smile at my husband who's standing by the entrance to the kitchen. He looks relaxed and confident and handsome. He's the kind of man you picture as your knight in shining armor, the courageous hero in a novel come to save the damsel in distress. So unlike …

I catch the direction of my thoughts and steer them back to safety. "Hungry?" I ask, wiping my hands on the towel hung over the oven handle.

He closes the space between us, loosening his tie. "Starving."

"Good. I made enough food to feed an army, I think."

I watch as William takes everything in, me standing by the stove, the dress I'm wearing, our wedding china sitting on the white granite, a crystal vase filled with white roses next to the plates. "Where's Evan?"

"He came in the morning, but I told him to take the rest of the day off. I made you dinner instead." I turn the stove off and walk into his arms. Standing on my tiptoes, I tilt my head back and grin. "We're celebrating."

"We are?" William places a quick kiss on the tip of my nose as his hands go to my hips. His fingers knead my skin and pull me flush against him, his touch warm and inviting. He lowers his head to my neck and shoulder, showering me with small kisses that stir my body awake yet my heart remains calm, unmoved. "Are you pregnant, my darling?"

Flushing, I shake my head. Since I got back from Paris, William reaches for me almost every night. He paints my body with kisses and his tongue while filling me with his seed.

"No, not that."

Needing to put some space between us, I go to retrieve the bottle of red sitting on the counter. With my back to him, I take a deep, calming breath. When I've schooled my features into a composed disguise, I turn to face him once more, pasting a smile.

"Remember all those floral design classes I took a while back?"

"Vaguely, but yes." William grabs a carrot from the salad and pops it into his mouth.

"I know I haven't said much about Paris, but during my stay there I helped an older gentleman at his flower shop." I smile, remembering Mr. Lemaire. "Obviously I didn't really know what I was doing, but it felt good to have a purpose. To *do* something. I'd like to think the experience changed me."

"What do you mean it changed you?"

"I'd like to do something with my time other than going to the gym and shopping and waiting for you to come home. There's absolutely nothing wrong with that. I'm lucky to have that choice, but that's not who I am." *It's who I thought I should be.* I stare at the bottle in my hands, tracing its label. "I want more. And, well, Evan mentioned during breakfast that his sister owns a flower shop in Rye." I hesitate, unsure of William's reaction. "I went to see her today, and she offered me a job as an apprentice slash assistant. Her name is Meg, and she's really, really lovely. Her place is—"

"Absolutely not."

About to pour wine into the glasses, the hand holding the bottle freezes in midair. "What did you say?"

William takes the bottle from my hand and fills our glasses. After chugging down his own, he adds, "This isn't Paris. Your place is at home. Think what our friends will say. What my grandmother will say. She already thinks I give you more than enough freedom."

I clear my throat. This can't be happening, not after everything has been going so well. *Maybe he's teasing me.* "You're joking, right?"

"No, not really." He shrugs. "Besides, I won't be made a laughing stock because my wife is some kind of lowly clerk at a random place."

He *has* to be joking. Any minute now he'll look at me, throw his head back, shouting with laughter. But seconds turn into minutes, and nothing happens. William's gaze holds mine captive, and I feel entrapped with nowhere to run. "What kind of caveman views are those? Next you're going to say that my job is to give you babies."

William sighs, running a hand through his golden hair, exasperation and annoyance radiate from his body. "That'd be a start. But it seems you can't even get that right."

I feel like he just punched me in the stomach. "This is where you apologize."

I'm met by hair rising silence.

I take a step back and look at him with revulsion and hurt before I turn away. "We're done here, William."

"No, we're not."

My skin breaks into goose bumps as soon as he comes to stand next to me. Taking my forearm in his hand, he stops me before I get a chance to escape. "Where do you think you're going?"

"Let go." I try to snatch my arm away from his hold, but he tightens his grip making it impossible for me to get away. "You're hurting me."

"Listen to me, and listen to me well." Gripping me by the chin, he makes me stare at him. His eyes, usually soft, are now hard as stone. "Tomorrow you're going to give this Meg a call and inform her you can't take the position anymore."

"Why would I do that?" I ignore the pain from his angry hold, a rebellion forming inside me. "I don't need your permission to do anything."

"You're my wife, and you're going to do what I tell you to do."

"No, I won't. You don't own me."

He tightens his grip even more, drawing closer to me. "Don't test me, Val." There's a dangerous edge to his tone that sends a chill running down my spine. I stare at William and feel as though I'm seeing him for the first time. He has the same features as the man I married. The man who's slept next to me for years. The man I promised to love and obey until death do us apart. But this man, with the mocking eyes and the cruel touch and the menacing words, is a stranger who frightens me. He can't be my William. But he is. And the thought that I might not know him at all leaves me reeling.

"You're scaring me," I say softly without looking away.

He lets go of me and pours himself another glass of wine, watching me closely.

Shaken, I grab the counter for support. After a few sips, he comes up behind me and places his hands on my shoulders. The uninvited touch sends chills running down my spine.

"I'm sorry, my darling. It's been a long fucking day and I lost my head." He kisses the curve of my neck, and I feel like I'm going to be sick. "Listen, I know it might not seem that way, but I only want what's best for us. Hell, you want a flower shop? I'll buy you one, and you can hire whomever you want. Now come, let's put this all behind us and go finish our dinner."

He takes my hand in his and guides us to the table. Numb and in a daze, I follow and sit on the chair next to his. Reaching for my napkin, I place it on my lap, and watch him fill my plate with salad. But my appetite is gone.

William sits down and reaches for his fork. "I thought you were planning my grandmother's ninetieth birthday? It's just around the corner." He smiles his golden boy smile, all charm and sweetness. He's back to being the William I know, and I could almost be fooled into believing I imagined the whole thing.

Almost.

"How about you focus on that party first, and when it's all over we can talk about this again?"

"Sure," I say listlessly, my gaze trained on his handsome profile before landing on the wall full of photographs behind him. Those perfect snapshots of our life. There's a wiry woman dressed in white standing next to a man. The picture perfect blushing bride. Her long brown hair surrounds her young face like a halo, and she's looking up at him adoringly as he smiles down at her. They look happy. In love.

A blindfold has been removed from my eyes as the image before me blurs through my tears.

Have I gotten it all wrong?

The next morning I'm coming back from a run when I notice two vans parked outside the front entrance and the doors to the house flung wide open. Slowing down, I frown as I follow a man carrying a huge bouquet of red roses inside. Mrs. Croft is standing at the top of the steps, her eyes glowing softly.

"Good morning, Mrs. Croft."

"Good morning, Valentina."

A different man walks past me at that moment, smiling politely as he goes down the steps toward the van.

I focus on Mrs. Croft. "What's going on? I don't remember placing an order for flowers."

Mrs. Croft smiles, maybe for the first time since I've known her. "Why don't you go inside and see for yourself?"

"Okay."

Stepping into the foyer, my eyes widen as I take in the view. Everywhere you look there are magnificent bouquets with dozens of red roses. The entire room is bursting with them. There's one particularly magnificent arrangement sitting on top of the maple table in the middle of the room. I lean toward it to smell the intoxicating aroma, noticing a note.

I'm sorry about last night.
I love you, my darling.

I accept his apology, but nothing feels the same. Nothing is.

CHAPTER TWENTY-EIGHT

SÉBASTIEN

"So why did you need me to get you an invitation to this party?" I hear Allegra say as I help her out of her coat.

I watch my agent, a very attractive woman in her mid-fifties, hand her coat to the young girl working the coat check tonight. She smiles kindly, reminding me that she can be nice when she wants to be. Known as one of the toughest agents to land in the art scene, she will stomp on your dreams without an ounce of remorse. But if you're lucky enough to catch her notice, you won't find a bigger advocate and supporter for your work. Allegra will either make you bleed or go to war for you.

She teases her silver gray hair, giving it some volume. "The Fitzpatricks aren't exactly your crowd. Very boring people."

I look around past a sea of guests, searching for her. "Does that make them more acceptable to you?"

"Of course," she says unashamedly. "God, I need a drink."

I grab two champagne flutes from a passing waiter and hand her one. "Here."

We clink glasses. *"Santé."*

"Santé." She takes a sip while studying me. "Have I told you you're my favorite client?"

"You have, but I'm sure you say that to all of your clients," I counter smoothly.

She laughs airily. "Just the handsome ones like you. But tell me, why did you want to come? And don't say it's because you wanted to celebrate Loretta's ninetieth birthday because I won't buy it."

I give my bowtie a tug. "I'm looking for someone."

"Oh?" Her interest sparks. "And who may that be?"

Back in Paris, all I had was a name and a town to go by. Valentina Fitzpatrick from Greenwich. Sophie came through for me, though. Greenwich high society was a small, incestuous pool. Her friend didn't know her personally, but they belonged to the same country club. Her husband golfed with William sometimes. Everything was relatively easy once I knew where to find her. I gave Allegra a call to ask her if she knew of the Fitzpatrick's. She didn't, but she'd heard rumblings about an upcoming party where the crème de la crème of New York and Connecticut would be in attendance. It was being hosted by Mr. and Mrs. William Alexander Fitzpatrick IV.

Allegra worked her magic and got us in.

When I first found out that Valentina had gone back to her husband, anger, hurt, and jealousy boiled inside me, burning me alive. But the same voice that kept telling me what we had was real urged me to go after Valentina. To not give up. She was planning to end things with her husband, so something must have happened to change her mind. It didn't make sense then. It still doesn't.

So here I am. Standing in Valentina's home with nothing but my heart to offer her. I want answers, and this might be my only chance. I clench my fists. I don't know where the night will take me, but one thing is for sure.

Tonight, I will leave this house either a whole or broken man.

I down the champagne in one large gulp as the image of Valentina dancing in my kitchen flashes before my eyes. "Someone I have unfinished business with."

"Ooh ... the plot thickens."

Allegra scans the room, studying crowds of people mingle amongst each other. We're about to move when she sees someone she recognizes and stops to chat with him. She introduces me to the man, but I can't recall his name, my attention elsewhere. My gaze follows every woman who resembles Valentina, hoping—dreading—to finally find her in a sea of meaningless faces.

And that's when I see her. My Valentina. Different scenarios of what our first encounter would be like kept playing in my mind since I stepped on the plane to New York, but none of them matter anymore. As my eyes drink her in, consuming her, all I want, all I need, is to hold her in my arms. To hell with her husband and the consequences. *She's mine. Mine.*

Valentina rushes down the grand staircase, bumping into some guests, apologizing to others.

Just as my feet begin to move of their own accord, I see a blond man following her close behind ...

CHAPTER
TWENTY-NINE

William

Earlier in the night ...

I HAVE TO GIVE it to Val. She sure knows how to throw a damn good party.

Wherever you look, people are having fun, enjoying the expensive caviar and champagne. A famous ballad singer croons one of his latest hits on the podium, an orchestra playing behind him. Loretta's ninetieth birthday party is in full swing, and even my grandmother won't be able to find one flaw in this evening.

Val stands next to me while I share skiing anecdotes with a group of our friends. Larry just got back from Zermatt in Switzerland and swears he won't ski anywhere else. As more people chime in with their own opinions, I take a moment to study my wife dispassionately. Hair swept in a perfect updo. Demure black gown. Eyes blank. How did I ever think she was full of life? There's nothing warm or inviting about her. Hiding behind a frigid calm, she's nothing but ice. No wonder I fuck around.

Gwyneth comes up to us and hooks her arm in mine. Smiling politely, she asks if I have a minute to talk to her, so I excuse myself from Val and our friends. I'm pretending to be a concerned brother, though there aren't any brotherly thoughts occupying my mind as I admire the way the skintight dress molds to her fucking gorgeous ass. Now *that's* a woman's body. We reach a hidden rose arbor where the grass is longer and its smell stronger. Relaxed, I sit on an iron bench.

Gwyneth follows me, a sinful tilt on her lips. "I see your plan worked." She sits next to me, her bare thigh touching mine, and raises a hand, letting her fingers slowly trace my thigh. She hides behind a cool, flirtatious veneer, but she can't fool me. She's jealous of Valentina. "You've got Val back."

"I do," I say, amusement in my voice. "And I don't think I've had a chance to thank you properly for that."

She leans toward me until her lips are tracing my jaw and her tits are pressed against my chest, her soft breath tickling my skin. "How about you thank me now?"

I lift her off the bench and pull her on top of me, her legs straddling mine. My cock's already hard. Hungry.

"You want me to fuck you like a whore?" I taunt, lifting my hips slightly, showing her how much I want her.

She groans, closing her eyes momentarily. "Yes, fuck me while your pathetic wife waits for you. Show me that you only want me and not her," she whispers huskily as she grinds her pussy against my erection.

"We can't right now," I murmur, peripherally aware of any sounds that could signal someone's arrival.

"What?" She pretends to pout. "Afraid to get caught?"

"Too much to lose." My hands go to her waist. "But you should know better, Gwyneth." I lean forward and bite her neck, making her cry in pain. "I only fuck her because I need to get her pregnant. Make her believe I'm a devoted husband." Loretta's threat of disinheriting me hangs in the air. Paris was a close call. I got comfortable, thinking that Valentina would never dare to leave me, and she almost did. Deep down in my bones, I know it. And I won't allow the same mistake to happen twice.

"What makes you think a baby will make her stay?"

"Because that's all she's ever wanted. She won't leave me after that."

She looks at me with some sort of perverse pleasure as she lowers a hand and strokes my cock over my pants. "I could give you one, too."

I throw my head back as her fingers begin to pump my dick. So damn good.

"I love you, William."

I grab her by the ass. "Kiss me so I can taste your words. Show me."

Right before I lose myself in my sister's kiss, I think of Valentina.

Yes … I've got her right where I want her.

I hear the crunch of leaves. Gwyneth and I both turn to our left at the same time and find Valentina standing there, horror and disbelief in her eyes.

"I—your grandmother wanted you …" Shaking her head, Valentina doesn't finish her sentence. She brings a hand to cover her mouth before turning on her feet and running toward the house as fast as she can.

"Fuck!" I push Gwyneth off my lap and stand. "Fuck."

Gwyneth, cool as always, flattens her dress, smoothing out the wrinkles. "Uh-oh. Someone's been caught being naughty," she taunts, laughing. "You better hurry, dear brother, and try to fix it. But somehow I get the feeling that this is even beyond your power."

I don't waste another second with Gwyneth. I hurry back to the house after Valentina. Blood pumps in my veins. Fear that she will ruin everything threatens to overpower me, but I push past it. I will find a way to fix this like I always do.

I can't lose her.

I won't.

CHAPTER THIRTY
Valentina

"I ONLY FUCK HER *because I need to get her pregnant. Make her believe I'm a devoted husband.*"

It was all a lie. A lie.

Feeling like I'm going to be sick, I run my hands along the length of my arms while trying to dismiss the sickening image of William and Gwyneth burned in my brain. I should be surprised, but I am not. Deep, deep down, some part of me must have always known it would come down to this. Sometimes we refuse to see the big fucking reality of it all because lying to oneself is much easier.

But I'm done.

I laugh bitterly. *My God, I have been such a fool.* They played me like a maestro, and I fell right into their trap, believing their lies with eyes wide open. The laughs they must have had at my expense.

I rush to the house, not caring about the party anymore. The noise. The people. It's all becomes too much. The need to be alone guides my step, propelling me to move faster.

In our bedroom, I go inside the walk-in closet, reach for a small suitcase, and begin to fill it with enough clothes to last me for a while. I don't know where I will go, but one thing is for sure, I can't stay here for another second.

"There you are," William says calmly. A tremor runs through me when I hear his voice coming from behind. I stop packing for a moment before I resume what I'm doing. *Don't look at him. I can do this. I can do this.*

"Val, darling, let me explain."

Oh, that's rich.

"Don't." Anger, sadness, disgust, confusion, and disappointment swirl inside me like a violent tornado, wrecking the home William and I built together, and shattering once and for all the paper-thin foundation of our marriage. "You don't need to explain anything to me. Keep the sordid details to yourself. I'm done."

I close my suitcase with trembling hands, reach for the handle, and head toward the door. I stop when I notice William reclining lazily against the doorframe. He watches me with a dangerous look in his eyes belied by a pleasant smile that sends chills running down my spine. Suddenly afraid, I tighten my grip on the suitcase.

"Please step to the side and let me through."

He crosses his arms and doesn't move. "Where do you think you're going?"

Without bothering to acknowledge his question, I try to get past him. William blocks the exit with his body. "When someone asks you a question, the polite thing is to answer back," he utters pleasantly.

"I don't owe you anything, much less an explanation." I raise my chin while quelling the fear rattling my bones. I feel off-balance as though my entire world has been tilted upside down. And as I stare at his easy smile and calm demeanor, anger bubbles inside me. Anger for all the years I've wasted on him and everything I have given up for him. But most of all, I'm angry with myself because I was too weak to walk away.

"What have I done to deserve this, William?"

He remains silent.

"I loved you so much. So fucking much I threw my pride away again and again," my voice cracks. "I let my love for you cripple and cut me. And you've watched me bleed without giving a shit. Well, I'm done handing you the knife."

"Listen to you finally showing your fucking backbone." He chuckles, his eyes dancing like pagan worshippers around a bonfire. He cups my cheek. The contact is so soft it would be easy to think that I imagined the caress. "Valentina ... Valentina ... What am I going to do with you?"

I take a step back, needing to put some space between us. "We're done. It's over. It's been over for a very long time."

"Quite the contrary, my darling." William is too quick for me. He snakes a hand behind my neck, gripping my hair in an unforgiving hold. "It's far from over. I own you. I own your body. I own your name. I own the clothes you're wearing. The air you breathe. You're mine and only mine," he hisses, tightening his grip, drawing closer to me.

"It's all smoke and mirrors," I say, rebelling against him and his words. "Just like you."

"Shut up," he orders menacingly.

I train myself to appear outwardly cool when in reality I'm struggling to just keep breathing. "I'm nobody's property. Do you hear me? Not anymore you disgusting—"

He slaps me hard with his other hand.

Stunned momentarily, I stare at this William with the cruel touch and stones for eyes and I realize I never knew him at all.

"Look what you've made me do," he adds calmly as though he's chatting about the weather.

"You've lost your mind," I say hoarsely before trying to shove him away, but it only seems to incense him more, make his hold tighter.

"Let go." I kick him hard, making William chuckle. "Get away from me."

"No." His grip grows more painful as a dangerous light glistens in his eyes. "You leave me no choice but to show you who you belong to."

His teeth crash against mine, taking my mouth in a possessive kiss meant to punish and debase me, but I end it by turning my face to the side. "Stop it."

"You've displeased me, Valentina." William ignores my pleas with a cold heart. He pushes me against the dresser, nudging my legs apart. "And when someone dares to displease me, they must be punished." His hands roam over my body, degrading me. His touch isn't soft or gentle. His caresses are meant to punish, to humiliate, to show me I'm at his mercy.

"William, no." I try to fight him off, but he's stronger, bigger than me. Panic rises inside me. "Don't do this, please. Stop."

William chuckles, not even breaking a sweat. "Look at you, getting all feisty."

At my wits' end, I start yelling for help, praying someone will hear me.

"Who do you think is going to hear you? They're all downstairs getting drunk." William laughs in my ear as he covers my mouth with his fingers. "Stop fighting me or I'll make it worse for you."

Little by little I'm losing control while handing it to William, and there's nothing I can do to stop him. He bunches my dress up around my waist, unzips his pants and takes out his cock. He rubs it against my entrance. Closing my eyes, I tune him out and what's happening around me. I grow numb as my mind takes me back to a magic night full of stars. Suddenly, it's not William who I feel or his punishing hands. It's Sébastien. He's dancing with me, filling my world with his beautiful light. And I'm loved and cherished once again.

"Ready?"

"Hmm?"

"Do you trust me?" he asks throatily, tightening his grip around my waist, pulling me closer to him.

I blink a couple times, still in a daze. However, the answer jumps out of me. "Yes."

No …

No …

No …

No!

The memory works like an electroshock awakening my mind from a stupor. I open my eyes, trying to push him off of me. "Stop."

William pulls closer, kissing my neck. "If you weren't so frigid, you might enjoy this."

"Stop." I push him again, barely moving him. "Stop!"

"It's your fucking duty after all."

Focus, Valentina. He doesn't get to win this. He doesn't get to take this from you. I pause. Close my eyes. Take a deep, calming breath. And when I'm ready, I shove him away with every ounce of strength I possess.

The force of my push takes William by surprise. He staggers back and trips on a chair, crashing on the carpeted floor.

As he's falling, I see a window of opportunity to escape. My ears ring as I make a move to cross the threshold. William tries to grip the skirt of my dress, but I am quicker than him.

"If you leave this room, I won't give you a cent," he shouts angrily, still on the floor. "You won't get my money, you hear me? You'll be back to being nothing. You're nothing without me!"

All this time I thought I was fighting for us, and now I realize I was fighting to be hurt over and over again, chasing memories that held us together. Love can't survive on memories alone. So I'm letting him go. It's time I forgive myself and the mistakes I've made. It's time I fight for me.

"I have given you my everything, William, and you've made me feel like there's nothing left of me. You've shattered me, broken me like I am made out of glass. Once. Twice. And each time I foolishly came back. Hoping it would be different, hoping you'd stay true to your word. Always hoping. Always blind. But you don't get to break me anymore."

I pause by the door, my entire body shaking compulsively. "I'd rather *be* nothing, *have* nothing, than remain married to you. I will have respect for myself, and that's all that matters."

My heart pounds in excitement as a light film of sweat covers my upper lip. Without giving William another thought, I rush out the room, leave him and this life behind running towards the front doors of the house. The only thought—my only goal—is to get away. I have nothing. No money. No clothes. But I don't care.

I am free.

I go down the stairs as fast as my feet will allow, bumping into some guests. When I've reached the landing, I stop to glance back and see William right behind, closing the space between us. Panic settles in the pit of my stomach. About to move again, I bump into someone and lose my balance.

Placing his hands on my forearms, the man stalls my fall. "I'm so sorry," I apologize distractedly, needing to move. "I wasn't looking where I w—" I raise my eyes.

My breath catches.

My heart stops.

The whole world disappears except the man who owns my heart and soul.

"Sébastien?"

He smiles softly, his eyes sad. "Hello, Valentina."

"What are you doing here?" I ask softly, afraid I'm dreaming and he's not really here.

"You took away my heart, and I want it back."

"Oh, Sébastien." I touch his face, my incredulous fingers aching to feel him, to make sure he is real. "I thought I lost you for good." His beautiful face blurs as a sob escapes my mouth, and I begin to cry. "I-I am so sorry for leaving you like that."

"Ma petite chouette." His hands tremble as he cups my cheeks. "My little love."

"I'm so sorry," I cry, unable to stop the tears from coming. "I'm so—"

Sébastien silences me with an everlasting kiss that breathes life into my soul. His splayed fingers strong against my skin feel as though he is trying to absorb me into him. Our mouths claim one another until we become two stars crashing and lighting up my night sky in magnificent, brilliant colors.

The kiss comes to an end, and my mind is still in a haze when I hear William say my name with utter hate. The room is so quiet, you could hear a pin drop.

My gaze finds William standing at the foot of the staircase not even ten feet away from us surrounded by friends and family. Loretta. Gwyneth. Larry. His shield. They all watch us with disapproval in their eyes. But I don't care what they think about me anymore. And the realization is one big high.

Loretta's icy glare bounces between William and me. "This is unacceptable," she utters with disgust. "Someone explain to me what is happening right now."

"Why don't you ask William and Gwyneth?"

"Valentina! The library," William orders, his face growing red. "Right now!"

Once upon a time, I would have listened to him. His hold on me was that powerful.

But not now.

Never again.

"No." I shake my head. A slow smile grows from within me. Out of me. "I don't think I will, actually. I'm done running back to you, William. We're over."

Sébastien takes my hand in his and brings it to his lips as he stares at William and Gwyneth and the whole lot, claiming me in front of them. Focusing on my husband, Sébastien dares him to come between us. To try and separate us, but William remains in his place. "Thought so," he says under his breath. Then he turns to look at me and grins like the rascal he is.

"Want to get out of here, ma petite chouette?"

And like that night in Paris when he whispered the same words to me, the same answer forms in my heart. "God, yes."

CHAPTER
THIRTY-ONE

BACK IN HIS HOTEL ROOM, the world and reality slip away. Words cease to matter. There is only silence, magical silence, and the wonderful man standing in front of me. I stare at him, my eyes swallowing his savage beauty for all the days, weeks, and months I have gone without him.

And he steals my breath away.

I was numb without him. My body dry. Parched. Lifeless. But as our gazes lock, my heart jumpstarts all over again. Beating harder. Faster. Life floods my veins. Sweet air fills my lungs. It is all because of him.

Nerves make my movements clumsy. My breathing is short and fast. Untamed happiness runs rampant within me. All that matters is the now. The present with him in it.

I don't know whether he comes to me or I go to him. All I know is that when his arms come around me, every cell in my body cries, *At last! At last!* I am lost and found in his sweet embrace.

Overcome by emotion, I look down at the floor, barely able to tell whether I'm standing or flying.

"Don't," he whispers hoarsely, tipping my chin up. "Don't look away from me ... I've gone too long without seeing you."

"Am I dreaming, Sébastien?" I brush his cheek. "I see you. I *feel you*. But I'm afraid. I'm afraid I'm dreaming. I'm afraid I'll wake up tomorrow and you won't be here standing in front of me. That I'll find myself back in a life without you. That—" my voice breaks, tears escaping. They are tears of joy and sadness because he is here. Because I have wasted so much time.

Sébastien catches one with his thumb. "I'm here." His hands tremble as he touches my face, his fingers trying to absorb my every feature, and all the love I see in his blue, blue eyes heals me like holy water. "I'm here."

"I thought ... after I left ... I thought that—"

"That I would never want to see you again?"

I nod.

"My little fool," he says hoarsely. "I came because I need you. Because I am nothing without you. I came because I love you. You hear me? I love you." He kisses me tenderly, recklessly, madly, senselessly. "I love you," he whispers between kisses that feel like small fireworks exploding and illuminating me from within. "And I am not going anywhere."

"Oh, Sébastien." And I kiss him back with everything I have, everything I am, consuming his words, his breath, his touch, as they become my benediction. *Heart, go easy on me,* I tell myself. But my heart replies, *This. This is life. This is love. Feel it all. Feel him and believe. Believe. Believe.*

We make it to the bed blindly, lying in it, and become all tongues and teeth and hands. Our clothes fall off of our bodies along with the past, the lies, the heartache. Leaving us naked, his bare skin against mine. His heart beating against mine. His taste bursting in my mouth. We kiss until our lips are bruised and raw, and then we kiss some more. In a life full of finite moments, I find infinity in him and his love.

When we come up for air, his body is on top of mine. His weight presses me down. He raises himself on his elbows and focuses on me with glowing and hungry eyes. His gaze roams my bare breasts, the tips red and hard because of his wanton touch. I rub his hardness in my hand, feeling its heat seeping into my palm, needing him inside me.

"I need you," I whisper huskily, wrapping my legs around his hips, pulling him closer to me.

"Wait. I just want to look at you." He pushes away a strand of hair off my face, "You're so damn beautiful." He runs a finger along my cheekbone, sending delicious shivers down my spine.

"Look at *you*," I say shakily, taking in every thick groove and muscle on his chest and every magnificent line of his face. He is a storm that invites you to dismiss your shelter and step outside so you can witness—feel—the beauty of his obliteration.

"Days and nights, I prayed for you to come to me. I prayed for one more glance of you. I imagined you dancing in my kitchen, on my bed as I made love to you." Sébastien slides down a little until his mouth covers my breast, sucks it in, flicking my erect nipple before biting it. Chills and more chills roll like waves throughout my body.

I reach for his hand and bring it between my legs where I need him the most. "Tell me more ..." I close my eyes, lick my dry lips as his thumb begins to rub my clit in slow, toe-curling, luscious circles. *My goodness, the man knows what he's doing.*

I moan as he slides back up and laughs in my ear. "Your knees raw. Your body full of me. I would fuck you until I'd marked every part of you. I wouldn't leave a place untouched."

He buries two of his fingers inside my soaked pussy, and I gasp at the intensity of his punishing yet divine touch. I tremble as he starts to pump into me, each time deeper and harder, driving me close to the edge of madness and want. He traces his tongue along my neck, tasting me.

"I would make you come with my mouth, with my cock and fingers inside your cunt, and you would love every single fucking second of it. Revel in it. And that's only the beginning of what I plan to do to you."

I half laugh, half moan when I lose his touch. He pulls his hand out of me and cups my face, his fingers glistening with my essence. I can smell my need for him as it soaks my skin, and I love it. I grab his head, pulling him closer to mine, feeling and tasting the sweetness of his breath touching my skin.

"Make me yours, Sébastien. Make me yours." I rub myself against his rock hard erection, my pussy covering him in my need. "Everything I am. This body. These hands. This heart. They all belong to you."

He kisses me as though my lips are the air he needs to live, and I kiss him for all the seconds, minutes, hours, and days without him. Pulling away, he grips my chin, makes me look at him as he raises himself on an elbow and drags the head of his cock along my opening with his hand.

"Say it again." He grazes my clit before sinking into me in one deep, hard thrust. Sébastien groans and bites my shoulder. Hard. I cry out in pain and pleasure, tilting my head back.

"Say it."

He thrusts hard.

"I belong to you."

He thrusts harder.

"Again."

Harder and harder.

"I belong to you."

He stops moving, my pussy contracting around him. "God sent you to me to give me life and to heal me." He fists my hair in his hands, and says huskily, "I had given up hope until you." Sébastien closes his eyes momentarily, opens them, and I can see they are glistening with unshed tears.

"You saved me."

I caress his cheek as a dam of sweet emotion breaks, and I drown in tenderness for this man. I wrap my legs tighter about his hips, kissing away his tears, his mouth, his chest. Everywhere. Wanting to memorize him and the feel of him.

"I love you so much, my beautiful man. It was always you. It has always been you."

"Fuck, Valentina," he utters, burying his face in my neck, and we lose ourselves in the violent rhythm of our fucking. He builds a church with his body in mine, making a sinner and a believer out of me while quieting my demons. Restraint gone, he shoots us into the stars until we reach the heavens and beyond. And when we fall and crash, we are reborn on the sheets of this bed. He fucks me savagely, claiming me over and over again—baptizing me in the holiness of his body, his kisses, and his love.

My name on his tongue and his taste on mine.

We come undone.

And when I feel his seed filling me, my body full with his cock, my skin burning with his kisses, I have never felt more whole. More complete.

Sébastien

Sometime during the night, I wake up to the sensation of kisses being showered all over my body. I open my eyes and find Valentina watching me, a soft smile on her lips.

"Hey."

"Hey."

We turn our faces to one another. I raise a hand to touch the curve of her mouth, noticing for the first time small changes in her appearance. She's slimmer. Her cheeks hollow. There's a trace of purple under her eyes. "I must've fallen asleep."

"Yes, you were tired."

"Did you sleep?"

She shakes her head, sighing. "When I came back, I woke up so many times in the middle of the night after dreaming of you, and ... well," she traces a shape over my heart, "that's when it hurt the most."

"I'm here, Valentina." I pull her into my arms, kissing her neck. I wish I could erase those memories, take her pain away and make it mine. "And I'm not going anywhere."

She buries her face in my chest and nods. "Steal me away. Take me to a place where we can start all over again. No past. No future. Just the present. Just you and me. Your body will be my shelter, my home. Can you do that?"

"The past cannot touch you anymore."

Seconds pass in silence.

"I know. I won't let it." She hesitates. "I need to explain Paris ... what happened tonight ..."

"Not right now." I take her hand in mine, bring it to my mouth, and kiss it. "You don't have—"

"No, please." She tightens her grip on my hand as her eyes implore me. "Let me explain. I want to explain and put this behind us once and for all."

"All right."

"William came to Paris asking me to forgive him and give him another chance. He seemed so lost and in pain. I wish I could've seen through his lies, but I was a fool. You see, I was living a lie, but that's all I ever knew. Lies. They were my reality. Or maybe I chose to be blind because I was afraid to open my eyes. I don't know. I felt so guilty, too." She lowers her gaze to our hands laced together.

"I thought, here is my husband suffering at my hand while I fell in love with you. It made me feel unworthy. Dishonest. I thought I had betrayed my husband. I wasn't in love with him anymore, but there was still love and commitment between us. A lifetime worth. Or so I believed. I didn't want to leave, but I thought I owed him my loyalty. I went back home to atone for my mistakes, to make it right by William."

When she says that she might still love him, jealousy makes me see red. Punch-a-hole-through-the-fucking-wall red. But then her next sentence cuts through the angry haze in my mind. I frown. "What do you mean by *or so I believed*?"

"I'm about to get there, and it gets really juicy." She chuckles sadly. "I came back to the States. To my life in Greenwich. And for a while, it seemed everything was working even though my heart wasn't in it."

"Why?"

"You know why."

"Say it." I grin. "I want to hear you say it."

She rolls her eyes, smiling nonetheless. "Because I loved you then. Because I love you now. Happy now?"

"Extremely," I say, feeling like I just won the Nobel Prize. I'm about to tell her to continue when the memory of coming home and finding her gone hits me in the chest like a grenade. So I ask her the one question that has kept me awake many nights wondering where it all went wrong. "Why didn't you say goodbye?"

"I tried. Before I left, I went to your apartment, but you weren't there."

"Sophie needed me to babysit her kids." I sigh, a sense of sorrow laying siege to my heart. "To think that maybe I could've—"

"Don't. Hindsight is twenty-twenty. It'll only drive you crazy to think like that. Trust me, *I know*." She gives me a quick peck on the lips. "Anyway, where was I? Oh yes, little cracks started to show."

Valentina tells me about William's reaction when he found out she wanted to work, and how things seemed to go downhill from there. What she overheard and saw happening between William and his sister at the party, and what happened in their bedroom. When she reaches that part of the story, it takes every ounce of power I own not to get out of this bed, go in search of that fucking piece of worthless filth, and destroy him. But the concern I see in her eyes calms me down.

She takes my hand, placing it on her cheek. "I wish I had been braver for you, for me, but at least something good came out of it. I finally realized what kind of man William truly is. I think I needed to see it to believe it and to wake up. If I hadn't, maybe I would've never broken free of the weird hold he had on me." She smiles. "So now I'm free. It's over. Truly over."

"I still would like to kill him," I rumble out, unsatisfied that the bastard got away unscathed.

"Don't. There's nothing more important to William than appearances. What happened tonight is punishment enough." She stares at me for a moment too long. "My God, I love you so much."

"Good," I say, dismissing William. He doesn't get to come between us anymore, not even his memory. "Because I need a lot of loving."

"Oh yeah?" She raises an eyebrow, a seductive light flashing in her gaze. "How much are we talking about here?"

"Oh, I don't know ..." I say, playing dumb, enjoying myself more than I should.

"Shall we play Hot and Cold to find out?"

"Now that's interesting ... How do you plan on—"

She smirks. She moves to kneel, encasing my hips with her legs, hovering over me. My cock stirs awake at the sight of her slim body branded by my hands and lips. She watches me, a sly smile on her face, as she glides her hands over her tits, touching her nipples and playing with them.

"Hot?"

I clear my throat. "Getting there."

"Oh yeah?" She leans on my chest as she lowers herself on my cock, and begins to rub her cunt on it.

"Hot?"

"Warmer," I groan, my hands going to her hips as she continues to torture me. But it's the reckless woman with laughter in her eyes that drives me to fucking perdition.

She taps her chin, seemingly thinking of her next play. "Hmm ..."

When she moves away from me to kneel next to my legs, I want to cry like a damn baby. "Come back and finish what you started, minx."

"Nope."

All coherent thought leaves my mind when Valentina takes my cock in her hand and brings it to her mouth, sucking and licking the head.

I curse slow and long.

"Warm?" she asks sarcastically, her lips grazing my dick.

"Fucking hell, woman." I cover my eyes with an arm. "You're trying to kill me."

"Maybe," she says, giggling. "Am I doing a good job?"

"I'd say."

She runs her tongue along my length slowly, making me feel every single torturous second of it. "Excuse me. I don't think I heard you. Did you say warm?"

"Hot," I breathe. "Hot."

She giggles.

"I thought so," she says before going to town, and fucking me with her mouth.

Yep, God is good.

CHAPTER THIRTY-TWO

Sébastien

"Sébastien?"

I caress her back, drowsy and content in the aftermath of our coupling. She's warm under my touch, and so delicious. "Hmm?"

"Talk to me about thunderstorms."

My fingers grow still. "Why they bother me so much?"

She nods.

"Remember what you said about the painting I gave you?"

She frowns. "Yes. It made me hurt for you."

"You weren't far off. That painting was about a woman I loved very much. Her name was Poppy."

"I see," she adds tentatively. "Can I ask what happened?"

I sigh, pulling her closer in my arms, trying to feel her around me. I need to know she's here now more than ever. "A drunk driver ran a stop sign. She didn't even make it to the hospital." I pause to sit up, running my hands through my hair. "She was a little over three months pregnant."

Valentina sits up as well and hugs me from behind. "I'm so sorry, Sébastien. So sorry."

"It rained all day, but it only got worse as I drove to the hospital. I was supposed to go with her, but something came up and I had to stay back in London. It should've been me, Valentina. Me. The man hit the driver's side. If I had been driving like I was supposed to, she would still be here. She deserved to live."

I stare out of the window, noticing dawn tinge the sky in soft pink, lavender, and vanilla colors. The eyes of my mind take me back to that day. "For the longest time, I wanted to die just so I could be with them. In my lucid moments, I waited day in and day out for them, expecting to wake up from a nightmare and find her lying next to me, her feet tangled around mine. And when she didn't come, I searched for her in my dreams. A smile. A glance. A sigh. It didn't matter. Sometimes I got lucky. Then the morning would arrive and with it the never-ending pain. The pillow would be soaked with tears and the sheets covered in my body's yearning."

Valentina tightens her arms around me and kisses my back. She doesn't say a word, and she doesn't have to. Just knowing that she's here is more than enough. It's everything.

"I didn't think I was going to make it."

"But you did, and that's what matters. And she isn't gone. Her memory lives." She lets go of me and shifts her position so she's straddling my lap. She places a hand over my heart. "She's here. And she will always be."

"What did I do to get so damn lucky?"

She kisses my nose. "I think it should be me asking that question."

I wrap her hair in my hand and make her look at me. "Come back to Paris with me. My flight leaves in two days."

"What?" She blinks a couple times.

"You have nothing keeping you here." I shower her face with kisses, needing to taste her. "Let's get out of New York and go back home."

She places her hands behind my neck, her fingers cradling the back of it. "But what about William? I need to get a divorce."

"Easy. You get a lawyer and deal with him over the phone. When you need to fly here to sign papers, you—"

"You're forgetting something."

"What's that?"

"I don't have nor want William's money, so I won't be able to pay for any of those things. My aunt left me enough to live modestly for a couple of months, and I will take that money because it's rightfully mine, but—"

"So you move in with me, and I'll pay for everything. God knows I have more money than I'll ever need."

She bites her lower lip, slightly shaking her head. "I can't let you do that for me."

"Is it the money?"

"Yes, that's part of it."

"Get your job back with Mr. Lemaire, and help me pay the bills then. I don't want to own you like that, Valentina. I don't want to be your jailer. I just want to love you freely and without any restrictions. I want to be your equal partner." I rest my forehead against hers. "I'm a simple man, Valentina. I don't ask for much. Just the woman I love in my arms, a warm bed, and a roof over us. Let me take care of you and love you," I add softly, wiping some of the tears starting to roll down her face. "That's all. For as long as you let me."

"You wonderful, wonderful man. But there's more. Most of my life I have depended on a man. Being with William has been my crutch." She catches herself and grins through tears. "*Had* been my crutch. I felt safe being married to him, and even though our marriage has been over for a very long time, I kept holding onto its safety net, onto him. But now that it's over, I need to prove to myself that I can stand on my own two feet and be fine. Learn how to fight my own battles rather than give in to fear."

"You don't have to fight alone, Valentina. I can be there for you."

"I know you would. However, this is my fight. One I must endure to make my way back to you. And going to Paris now, moving in with you ..." She gives her head a little shake while reaching for my hand before bringing it to her lips and kissing it. "I love you so much, Sébastien. But I need time to sort things out, to regroup and figure myself."

I hear what she's saying. Hell, I even understand where she's coming from, but it doesn't make it hurt any less. Placing my hands on the back of her head, I draw her toward me and kiss her with everything I've got. With all the desperation coursing through me, it's a kiss that says, *I'm letting you go not because I want to, but because I have to. And because I know you will come back to me. I will. I will come back to you. Wait for me. Wait for me.* The kiss comes to an end, leaving us emotionally battered. "I feel like I just got you back and I'm already losing you."

"You're not losing me." She grabs my hair and makes me look at the truth in her eyes. "It's only time. And we will be stronger for it."

"Are emails out too?" I joke, trying to lighten the mood but at the same time scared to death that this might be it.

"No, they aren't." She tries to smile even though it seems as though she's on the verge of tears again, the pain too raw.

We hold onto each other, not wanting to let go, both of us realizing that all we have left are these hours together. But that's life for you. It certainly never plays fair. I could move to New York City to be near her, but that wouldn't be right. She's asking me for space and time, and I will give her both even though it feels as though I'm chopping off my own arm. The memories made in the four walls of this hotel room will have to do. They will become the bread to feed our hungry souls in the days to come when an aching emptiness carves holes in our bodies.

Her eyes land briefly on the outline of a skyscraper outside the window before locking with mine again. There's a rush of color in her cheeks. A new bright light in her gaze. "I've got it! All right, movie time."

"*Really*, Valentina?"

"I promise there's a point." She laughs and kisses me at the same time. "Have you ever watched *An Affair To Remember*?"

"Now you're talking."

"I knew I'd eventually find a movie we both love," she says, chuckling. "You know how Cary Grant and Deborah Kerr's characters agreed to meet at the top of the Empire State Building in six months if their feelings remained the same?"

"Mhmm, but we all know how *that* turned out."

"Shh." She kisses my lips. "If things haven't changed for you," she kisses my eyes, "meet me at the top of the Eiffel Tower in six months." She kisses my cheeks. "Shall we make it 2:00 p.m.?" She kisses my mouth, and it tastes like goodbye and hello and someday we will meet again. It also tastes like hope and a new beginning.

"Six months, huh?"

She nods while spreading needy kisses along my jawline. "We'll have this, our love." She rolls her hips against me, her warm pussy spreading for my cock. "No one will take that away from us."

I nudge her with my growing erection, needing to fuck her and own her. "I'll wait for you," I growl in her ear before biting it.

"Good." Valentina smiles, and in her smile I see the whole future spread in front of us. "Now stop talking and fuck me."

"With all my fucking pleasure."

I remove Valentina from my lap, flipping her on her stomach as she squeals, and straddle her. As I rub my cock between her ass cheeks, I lean over, trailing kisses on her spine, watching little bumps rise. I reach her neck and trace the salty skin there with my tongue.

"Have you ever been taken here?" I ask, teasing her little hole, feeling it contract under my thumb.

She groans, fisting the sheets. "N-No ..."

I bring a hand to my mouth, lick two fingers, and go back to taunting Valentina in that sweet spot. I rub it in small circles until slowly guiding one digit past her resistance. I begin to move my finger in her ass, going deeper and deeper.

"Do you want me to take you here?"

"Oh, God," she moans, and it makes my cock rock hard.

I continue to torture her by adding another finger, plunging them inside her. Slow and fast. Shallow and deep. Her cunt contracts around me as I curl my fingertips against her wall and finger fuck her to hell and back.

"Do you want me fucking your sweet ass?"

"I ..." She moves her head side to side, pushing her ass up, seeking relief. "Yes, just take me, please. I can't wait any longer. Please, Sébastien ..."

She cries when I drag my fingers out of her. My hands leisurely travel the lines of her shoulder blades, spine, down to her hips. Our breathing becomes labored, hungry for more. I'm spreading her ass ready to penetrate her ...

I freeze.

Fuck.

"What's the matter?" Valentina asks breathlessly, glancing over the shoulder, looking like a pagan queen. Her burning gaze meets mine. "Why did you stop?"

"I have no lube," I say, cursing my luck.

She laughs shakily. "Do I need it?"

I chuckle, patting Valentina's gorgeous ass. "I'm afraid so."

"Can't you use something else?"

"I don't—" Then I remember the little bottle of lotion sitting next to the shampoo in the bathroom. I look up at the sky and utter a quick thank you. "Be right back. Don't move," I say before leaning down and biting her ass.

I come back to find Valentina propped on her forearms, long brown hair running down her ivory body. Fire on her cheeks. Stars in her eyes. Swollen lips branded by me. She smiles invitingly, taunting me, seducing me. *Jesus Christ. The woman is going to be the death of me.*

"Found what you need?"

Climbing the bed, I place the bottle next to me. "Yeah."

I slide down and kneel at the altar of Valentina's body, ready to make my communion. Leaning down, I cover her body with sizzling kisses until I reach the inviting curve of her ass. I spread it and drag my tongue from the little pucker down to her soaked pussy.

"So damn sweet," I say, breathing her in, wanting to make the moment last.

She grinds her hips as she looks over her shoulder, watching me kissing, probing, and lapping her tight hole. Her eyes roll back as she bites her lower lip. She curses, begging me to take her, to put her out of her misery.

"Not yet."

I spread her ass cheeks wider and bury my face in them, fucking her with my tongue.

"Please … no more … I need you now," she begs, whimpering.

"What do you need? Say it."

She groans. "Your cock. Inside me. Take me, please."

Sweat covers both of our bodies. The glass windows are fogged. The sheets are discarded on the floor. The smell of our fucking fills the room.

This is life.

This is beauty.

I move on top of her. Reaching for the lotion, I open it, pour some on my palm, coating my cock with it, and throw the bottle away. Anticipation makes my brain hazy. I give my dick a few pumps and bring the head into her tight ass, pressing the head slowly between her open cheeks.

"Fuck," Valentina cries.

"Do you want me to stop?" I ask, the words torn from my chest, watching her take me in little by little. The feel of her body accepting me and watching it take me is like dying a slow, beautiful death.

"No, don't stop." Back arched, she presses against me. "I need more …"

"Almost there," I say hoarsely, trying to reel myself back. Take it slow when all I want to do is fuck her to oblivion.

"Please …"

It's her words that makes me lose it. Grabbing her by the hips, I push all the way in. I close my eyes and throw my head back, feeling like I'm about to shoot my load inside her. There are no words to explain the sensation of her tightly wrapped around me.

"You okay?"

She nods. "Yes, oh, God. But I want you deeper. I want more."

I chuckle as I grab her hips, push her forward, and start to pump into her. At first I take it slow, my thrusts shallow. I pull back just enough to leave the tip of my cock inside her and then push aggressively into her, hard. Over and over again.

"Harder …" she pleads. "More."

"Fuck, Valentina," I groan.

The bed frame rattles as the force of my thrusts increases, pounding Valentina harder and faster each time, wanting to ruin her completely. I reach under and begin to rub her clit while fucking her cunt with my fingers. Her moans turn into screams.

I grab her hair in my fist and pull her head back toward me. "I give you six months, you hear me?" I growl in her ear. "Six months." I wrap my hand around her neck and kiss her savagely on the mouth as I take and demand. And my beautiful Valentina, my gorgeous woman, gives me everything I want. She willingly surrenders her body and soul to me.

"That's all I need," she breathes brokenly. Rubbing her own clit, she starts to spasm around me as our rhythm becomes more desperate. More needy. *More everything.* So close to the edge, I let the beast inside me loose and fuck her as hard and as fast and as shamelessly as I possibly can until we both come undone. We fly so fucking high we reach nirvana. A ragged groan escapes my lips as my seed spills inside her, and she comes shouting my name.

Ah.

There it is.

Total surrender.

I own her like she owns me.

And no amount of time or distance will come between us.

CHAPTER THIRTY-THREE
Valentina

The next morning ...

Half asleep, my arms search for Sébastien but come back empty, finding nothing but a dent where he should be lying. I sit up and yawn, dismissing the last traces of sleep.

"Sébastien?"

I glance around the room searching for him, but it appears he isn't here. The bathroom door is open and the lights are off. The small desk by the window is empty and so is the couch across from the bed.

Weird.

Wondering what time it is, I turn to look at the clock on the nightstand table when my eyes land on a sheet of paper with the hotel's logo propped against the phone. My fingers as though they had a life of their own immediately reach for the note.

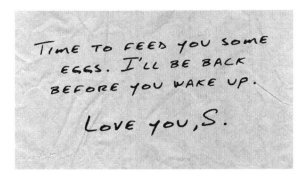

TIME TO FEED YOU SOME
EGGS. I'LL BE BACK
BEFORE YOU WAKE UP.

Love you, S.

Grinning, I throw myself back on the bed and stretch my arms. My body is sore and satiated, but I'm full of crazed energy. *We will be fine. I know it.* Last night (or earlier this morning) when he asked me to go back to Paris with him, I was so tempted to say yes. I still am. After all, nothing could make me happier than to finally be with him without any worries and boundaries, and to be able to love him. Just love him. But deep down I know, especially after what happened with William, that I need to take some time for myself before I jump back into another relationship. I need to figure out what I want to do with my life. Learn who Valentina is when she isn't an extension of the man she happens to be with at the time. And even though I love Sébastien with all of my heart, I need to make sure I'm with him because I *want* to be and not because I *need* to be. Only then will I be able to give him my love, and both he and I will know that it is given freely and without conditions.

I look at the note in my hands and smile knowing that we are doing the right thing.

Our love will find a way.

After placing the card on the table, I get up and head to the bathroom, ready to take a shower. I'm turning the water on when I hear a knock at the door. I frown. Maybe Sébastien left his key in the room. I turn the water off and grab his white shirt, putting it on before going to the door.

"Coming!"

"Did you forget your ke—" I open the door in a rush of excitement and happiness, but my smile disappears when my gaze connects with green eyes.

"Hello, darling. Miss me?"

And just like that, I know it is over …

CHAPTER THIRTY-FOUR
Valentina

My aunt used to say that if you wanted to know how a person *truly* felt about you, just look in their eyes, and find your answer because eyes are the windows to the soul.

William has the kind of charming eyes that invite you to fall in love with them. He laughs, and they shine. He kisses you and they burn. He makes love to you, and they shatter you. They can make you believe *anything* he wants you to. For they are as deceiving as they are beautiful.

Just like him.

However, he doesn't hide behind lies anymore.

As he stares at me, all I see is pure, naked hatred scorching the green forest of his eyes.

"Aren't you going to invite me in?" he asks pleasantly.

I lick my lips, suddenly dry. "How did you find me?"

"I tracked your phone."

He takes a step forward.

I take a step back, a shiver running down my spine.

Don't show fear.

Don't.

Don't.

"I don't know why you bothered coming all the way here. Like I said the other night, we're done."

"Oh, *really?*" He smiles then, a soulless smile, and it chills me to the bone.

"Yes," I say, feeling ensnared by him. "Please go before I call security."

"And have them do what? You're my wife." Before I know what's happening, he wraps his hand around my neck holding it in a vise-like grip. "You thought you could escape me, huh?"

He shoves me inside the room, kicking the door closed behind us, and slams me against the wall. The air leaves my lungs, his grip growing more painful. "You thought you could dismiss me just like that, you fucking whore."

"Please, William ..." I claw at his hands around my neck. "Let go. I can't breathe."

"You made me a laughing stock in front of our friends and family." He slams me harder, tightening his grip around me. "If you had only listened to me none of this would be happening. But no, you had to play the victim card. *Poor* little Valentina ..."

With each second that passes, William's anger grows and grows. Scared to death of what he will do to me, I try to reason with him. "William," I say, closing my eyes momentarily as the room spins, growing dizzy with the lack of oxygen. "You don't have to do this. L-Let's talk ... please."

But William is lost in the jungle of his madness, his once handsome features marred by hatred. "You know this is all your fault. If you weren't so frigid, I wouldn't have to fuck other women." His grip loosens a bit as he drops his gaze down to my body, his eyes roaming the outline of my breasts imprinted on the dress shirt. He snakes a hand under the shirt, his fingers finding me naked where I'm sore, and still full of Sébastien.

"Whore," he says quietly and sweetly, his voice vibrating with pure hatred. He brings that same hand to his face and smells me on his skin. "You've been fucking him behind my back all this time, haven't you?"

"No ... not like that," I try to say, but the words come out like a whisper.

Slowly and deliberately he squeezes my neck. "There's nothing sweeter than gazing into your eyes as I drain the life out of you."

"I can't breathe ..."

Everything becomes hazy...

LOVE ME IN THE DARK

No.

William doesn't get to win this.

I repeatedly blink as my ears ring, feeling an adrenaline rush. My fight-or-flight response kicks in at full force, and I start to thrash, trying to free myself from him, but he's too strong.

I knee William in the groin, making him fall to the ground and howl in pain. But before I get a chance to escape, William grabs me by the ankle and I tumble onto the floor. He's on top of me trying to rip my shirt off and pressing the bulge of his erection against my core when we hear bottles shattering. Our gazes move to the door, and we find Sébastien standing there, his chest rising and falling at rapid speed, thunder and hell on his face.

And as I desperately drink him in, he reminds me of a fallen angel coming to punish those who have sinned. Sébastien closes the space between us in two ground-eating strides and throws him across the room. "Get the fuck away from her," he utters with seething dislike.

William stands up immediately, straightening his clothes. "You're welcome to her," he says, stepping away from us. "The bitch is of no use to me anymore."

Sébastien goes straight for William's middle. The two of them fall to the ground. He starts to brutally punch William in the face and his sides and every single inch he's able to reach. William at first tries to deflect his blows, but Sébastien is much bigger and faster and angrier than him.

"Sébastien, please, he's not worth it. Stop!" I beg, gasping for air. But he's so far gone in his desire to punish William that my words don't get through to him. *Think, Valentina. Think. You must stop this.*

Throwing caution to the wind and not caring that I could get hurt, I crawl toward Sébastien and touch him on the back. "Please, my love, he's not worth it. Let him go. Come back to me." The moment my hand comes into contact with him, he stiffens and turns to look at me, a crazed expression in his eyes.

"Come back to me, Sébastien. Come back."

"Valentina." Sébastien blinks, and it's like he comes out of a trance. He moves away from William, who's lying like a pile of dirt on the floor, stands up and takes my hand gently in his, pulling me into his arms. "Are you all right?" He touches me everywhere, searching for injuries. "Did he hurt you?"

"I'm okay," I say through the burning pain in my neck, wrapping my arms around him. "I'm okay."

We hear William groan then, drawing our attention back to him. He's rolling on the floor holding his stomach, bruises forming all over his bloodied face.

I cling to Sébastien, stopping him from going back to finish his obliteration of the useless man next to us.

"Valentina ..." Sébastien's gaze bounces from me to William and back to me, appearing torn. Then he focuses on my neck, and a guttural sound escapes his mouth. "Your neck, Valentina. He fucking hurt you. I'm going to kill that son of a bitch."

"Please. Sébastien. Stay with me," I beseech him with my voice, with my hands, with everything I have, while holding onto him. "Let him go. He's not worth it."

Sébastien stills, nods and then looks at William. "If you so much as come within five hundred feet of her, I will fucking kill you. Now get the fuck out of here before I finish you, you son of a bitch."

For the first time since I met him, I see fear in William's eyes. He repeatedly nods as he struggles to stand. Once he's on his feet, he runs out the door and never looks back.

"Hey, eyes on me," Sébastien says. Spellbound, I watch him cup my cheeks, his fingers so gentle it makes me want to weep. A strand of hair falls forward and partially covers his worried eyes as he studies my face. "Are you sure you're okay?"

I look at the door, William gone from the hotel room, from my life forever, and then focus on Sébastien's dear face. I cover his bruised fingers with mine, my entire body shaking as all the love I have for this incredible, beautiful man rushes through me like a river of spring water, purifying me.

As our gazes lock, I know that I will be okay.

I will get there.

I will rise again.

I will stand on my feet amongst the ruins of my life and rebuild myself. If I cut myself along the way, I will bear those scars proudly for they are mine. They are proof I didn't give up. I fell. Got up. Tried again. I will continue to do so until I get it right. And my love for this man will be the light illuminating my path as I make my way back to him.

"Yes. I will be."

CHAPTER
THRITY-FIVE

Six months later ...

"So are you nervous?" Gigi asks over the phone. "Today is Valentina-finally-gets-laid-again day."

I smile at the outrageous comment. After news had broken that William and I were getting a divorce, I found an ally and friend in Gigi. We became very close even though I wasn't a part of that world anymore. She introduced me to Charlie, her lawyer, who was a miracle worker. No matter how good William's lawyers were, Charlie and his team were ten times better. The divorce proceedings went smoothly, or as smooth as they could possibly go when it came to William and his family. Gigi mentioned some scandal about Loretta disinheriting him, but like a cat, he landed on his feet and is now dating a wealthy socialite. *Poor woman.*

I shake my head, dismissing William from my mind. He's the last person I want to be thinking of today, *or ever.*

"Take a guess."

"How many times have you changed?"

"Uh ... why do you ask?" I grip the phone tighter and look at the pile of clothes lying on the bed, cringing a little.

"Because I know you, babe."

I sigh. "Five times."

She laughs throatily. "Oh, Val, when are you going to learn? You could probably wear a sack of potatoes, and Sébastien wouldn't care. He's just going to take it off anyway."

I blush as memories of those two idyllic days spent in his hotel room replay in my head. "God, I hope you're right."

There's a pause, and I know what she's going to ask before she even utters the words.

"Have you heard from him?"

"Not since the last email …"

About four months ago, Sébastien sent me an email. He wrote in it that he had met a man through Sophie who was looking for an artist to paint a set of portraits of people living in remote places of rural China. The man himself was Chinese American and wanted to honor his heritage. He also happened to be one of the wealthiest men in the world, so he could afford to commission a world-renowned artist to paint these portraits. Sébastien wanted to do it. Not because of the money, but because he was interested in learning and visiting those gems of civilizations hidden away in the mountains of China. The only thing that made him waver in his decision was that he wouldn't be able to get in touch with me for a couple of months. The places he'd be visiting didn't have Internet or phone lines.

I knew Sébastien wanted to do it. I had never heard him so excited. And even though every part of me revolted to the idea of not hearing from him for months on end, I also wanted him to be happy. I told him he was crazy for even thinking about it. *Take the job,* I wrote. *I will be here waiting for you. Waiting for October 5th and 2:00 p.m. to come.*

The last time I had heard from him was three months ago when he landed in Beijing. Instead of emailing like we had agreed upon, he called. We stayed on the phone for hours talking about everything and nothing at all. Just like how it had been in Paris, but lovelier, far lovelier. Also, there's something to be said about phone sex. We fell asleep listening to each other that night, the distance becoming a meaningless nothing for some brief, halcyon hours.

Life went on …

And three months later here I am, missing him with an ache in my soul. Whenever my mind begins to drift away with maybes and what-ifs, I shut it down. Fear is one big bitch, but turns out I'm an even bigger bitch because I am done, *done*, letting it control me.

"But he'll be there." I stare at my reflection in the mirror. The woman looking back at me stands tall and proud. She earned it. She worked hard to get here. She smiles, her eyes glowing. "I know it."

"That's the spirit."

My eyes land briefly on the clock hanging on the wall, noticing the time. 12:45 p.m., and my heart skips a beat. "All right, Gigi. I have to go."

"I want all the filthy details later." She pauses, sobering up. "Good luck, my friend."

"Thank you. Oh, before I forget, I told Linda she could have the weekend off."

"Already got it under control. I'm going to cover her shift at the store."

"Wait, what?"

"It's my store, too, you know? And I'm bored. I figured I could help a little."

Soon after Sébastien left, I started working for Megan at her flower store in Rye. I learned a lot from that experience. Then one day she came in and told me she was moving to San Francisco. She was done with long distance relationships and was ready to follow her boyfriend there. *Don't think for a moment I didn't see the irony in that.* She asked if I would be interested in buying the store. I had my aunt's money, and I had been living frugally since leaving William, but my savings were nowhere near the asking price. I was venting about it to Gigi when she surprised me by offering to be my partner and investing the missing amount of money. I knew what she was doing, and I was tempted to refuse her help. I wanted to prove to myself I could thrive on my own. But she made some valid points. She had a lot of money and saw a good investment in me. It couldn't hurt her, and we would both benefit from it. I ended up accepting. A month later, we were the proud owners of La Bohème Flowers.

"Of course. I love it," I say.

She chuckles ruefully. "Don't get used to it. Now go. Even *I'm* starting to get nervous."

We say goodbye and hang up. I take one last look at my reflection, butterflies in my stomach. "Ready, Valentina?"

Never been more ready, my heart answers.

I laugh, excitement and nerves running freely in my veins. Reaching for my bag, I leave the hotel where I'm staying and go in search of my future.

But it seems like fate has other plans for me. First, we hit tons of traffic. On the way there, the taxi gets into a car accident. I get out of the car and leave the taxi driver and the angry car owner yelling at each other. Now running very late, I try to look for another taxi. I find one by pure luck. *Okay, maybe fate doesn't hate me after all.* I get in and tell the driver where to drop me off.

I look at the time.

1:55 p.m.

Shit.

I realize I'm not going to make it on time, and it makes me want to cry. *What if he leaves when he doesn't see me there?* I reach the Eiffel Tower with my prepaid ticket, get in line and take the elevator all the way to the second floor. I rush out, and I'm immediately surrounded by hordes of people. It's now 2:20 p.m.

Desperation boils inside me as I look around trying to find a man with the devil in his eyes. Then I see him. My ears ring. He's standing on the other side with his back to me. He's watching the city. If my heart could fly out of my body, it would be all the way in the sky right now. I go to him, tap him on the shoulder, ready to jump him or kiss him. He turns around, and my heart drops as the stranger stares back at me. I apologize, a false smile on my lips.

2:20 p.m. turns into 2:30 p.m.

As more minutes pass, I keep repeating inside my head that he will come. He will be here. Maybe he hit some traffic, too. Numb, I wrap my arms around myself, trying to hold onto the hope inside. I forbid it to escape from the cage of my bones.

I sigh. My shoulders drop. The sounds of people laughing and talking around me disappear. Then, I remember the top floor. What if he misheard me? *Oh my God, maybe that's it.* I run to the elevator, pressing the button to go up a few times. The elevator arrives. A large group of people gets out.

Except for one.

My entire body starts to shake. My heart explodes in a kaleidoscope of emotions, bursting out of me. His worried gaze locks with mine, and he smiles tenderly. And there it is. Hope, love, happiness exploding from everywhere in me and out of me.

I feel like I'm about to faint. "Sébastien," I say softly, his name barely a whisper.

"Hello, Valentina."

My knees give out as Sébastien steps out of the elevator and takes me in his arms, wrapping me in an all-encompassing embrace that swallows me whole. He breathes me in as a tremor rolls over him, and I breathe him. And all the months without each other fall away.

"You came," I cry, gripping his shoulders hard, afraid to let him go. "You came!"

"Of course I came." He caresses my wet cheek as he smiles softly into my eyes. "I waited here for a while, but when you didn't come, I thought maybe I got the floors wrong and went to the top one to look for you."

"There was an accident," I say, trying to explain my delay.

He groans. "*See*, I told you."

I smile through the tears in my eyes. "So this is how our story ends?"

"No, ma petite chouette." He smiles back. "This is how our story begins."

The end.

ACKNOWLEDGEMENTS

I WANT TO THANK MY husband and family for loving me and supporting me through it all. I love you more than words can ever describe.

Next I would like to thank each and every single person that helped me in creating Love Me in the Dark—my very special group of ALPHA readers. Without your help and feedback this book would have never been completed. Luna, Joanna, Katherine— LMitD wouldn't be what it is without you! So I thank you so much for holding my hand during all those sleepless nights when I wanted to give up and throw in the towel. You were right there, putting your lives on hold just so I could have your feedback as soon as possible. You guys came through for me, and, honestly, I can easily say that this book is as much yours as it is mine. I love you, girls.

Rachel, Megan, Melissa, Deanna, Terilyn, Christy, Teri, Alissa, Mo, and Mint- thank you soo much for beta reading this book! Your feedback made this book! I appreciate you and love you <3

Jennifer, my beautiful and talented editor, thank you so much for being there for me and for dealing with my crazy. I wrote Love Me in the Dark, but it was your work and magic that made it readable and enjoyable. THANK YOU.

Melissa Saneholtz, thank you, thank you, thank you!!! Thank you for dealing with my crazy, for keeping me in check, and for basically taking care of everything while I wrote. You're the best publicist ever.

Penelope, Ava, Claire, Leigh, Corinne, Syreeta, Raine, and all the awesome authors I'm lucky to call friends. You guys are my tribe. <3

Marla, I want to thank you for perfecting LMitD with your proofreading services. It was a pleasure working with you!

Layla, thank you so much for helping me with Sébastien's French and all the translations.

Mo, I might steal you from Syreeta if you continue to be that awesome.

Kassi, thank you so much for making EV pretty and for answering all my questions. You were always there for me when I had a question with regards to the formatting, and, as always, your work is exceptional and reliable.

Hang, the cover you created for Love Me in the Dark took my breath away—It's perfect. You're so amazingly talented and patient! You have a client for life!

I want to give a special shout out to all the bloggers and readers that helped spread the word. No one would know about my novel if it weren't for your help. I would be nothing without your help. Thank you for believing in me (again) and in LMitD. MAD LOVE TO YOU ALL!

Also, special thanks to Kylie and Give Me Books for organizing a kick-ass cover reveal and blog tour. You ladies are so wonderful to work with. Also, thank you to Lisa from The Rock Stars of Romance. Bethany from The Book Bee and Cheri from Kindle Crack, thank you so much for your support! Big thank you to Angie from Angie's Dreamy Reads, Jenny and Gitte from Totally Booked, Yamara, Shayna, Kcee, Yvette, Sophie, Christy! And sooo many amazing bloggers and readers! Love you, guys!

Thank you to all my family and friends for putting up with me and for always being there for me. I know I'm forgetting someone and if I do know that I'm truly sorry. I love all the encouraging words, the lovely words from every single person that has stopped by my page and said hello. I love every single one of you.

This book would not be anything without the support and love from all of you. Thank *you* so, so much.

MIA'S LINKS

Read an excerpt of

Easy Virtue
by Mia Asher

CHAPTER ONE

What is love?

I don't know.

I've never had it.

Is it even real?

No, I don't think so. I mean, how can I believe in love when I've never witnessed it? When it seems to only exist in books and films, or in the lives of people more fortunate than me? *Trust me, I know.*

Love is my personal chimera.

I am gazing at brown eyes, admiring the richness of the color, the beauty of the man to whom they belong.

"You're so beautiful, Blaire ... so wet," he murmurs, his hand going between my legs as he begins to rub me. The soft invasion of his fingers spreads me open, tuning my body to his wants and needs, preparing me to be taken as the hot friction of his touch lights a wildfire within my body. It's not the first time he has touched me like this, but each time feels better and better—the sensations all consuming and heady.

One finger.

Two fingers.

One finger.

Two fingers.

Over and over again.

His invasion is fast and slow, deep and shallow. His touch is soiled heaven.

As I open my legs wider for him, I wonder if it feels this good because of him, or because I'm taking something that doesn't belong to me and making it mine.

"Don't stop ... it feels so good," I breathe.

Okay, maybe it's because at this moment in time *this man* thinks he loves me and no one else but me, however false his proclamation may be.

I close my eyes as his lips land on mine. He kisses me gently, as if I'm made out of glass. He kisses me with that familiar mouth I've seen smile tenderly at me so many times before. The assault of his tongue debilitates me but doesn't incapacitate me.

"It's four dollars, gorgeous," the cute barista says, smiling at me.

I'm about to pay for my cappuccino when I hear a deep, manly voice say, "Let me get that for you."

A man wearing a beige suit comes forward, standing next to me as he hands the barista some bills. "I've seen you around ... you're Paige's friend."

I smile, licking my suddenly dry lips. "Thank you, and yes ... I know Paige."

The smile on his handsome face seems to freeze as his gaze follows the tip of my tongue, the spark of hunger brightening his eyes. Inwardly, I smile because who knew it was so easy to make men desire me, particularly when I went without attention for so long.

"My pleasure. Are you"—he coughs—"here with someone else?"

I shake my head and look at him through fluttering eyelashes. "No, I'm here by myself." I pause, touching his arm invitingly, and smile. "Would you like to join me?"

He looks around the coffee shop, probably considering if he should, if it's proper to do so, but less than five seconds later, he's staring at me once again. "Sure."

Yes, just like that.

The beige walls are spinning.

The clock is ticking.

The bed springs creak as the moon shines outside the motel window.

And the man above me kisses me while he fingers me, preparing me for him. *Gotta love such a thoughtful man.*

I can taste his sweet saliva mixing with mine, and I love it.

"Please," I beg against his lips, reaching for his hard cock and wrapping my fingers around it. "I'm ready."

I feel his mouth leave mine as he begins to make his way down my partially dressed body. "Are you sure, Blaire? Are you sure you want to do this with me?"

I open my eyes to witness what I think I want him to do. No, what I'm *sure* I want him to do. I can't help the smile I feel playing on my lips as I see him struggling with his conscience. He asks me if I'm sure when he has already fucked my mouth with his cock countless number of times, when his fingers have filled every orifice of my body. Should I laugh? No ... I decide to take pity instead.

"I'm sure, so sure," I say, letting my arms land like dead weight on the bed, the cheap fabric rough against my skin.

"All right."

When I feel the bed dip between my legs, I instinctively open them for him and watch as he brings a condom package to his mouth. As he rips it open with his teeth, I admire his perfect full lips that emphasize how good-looking he is.

I feel pleased with myself.

So fucking pleased because he wants me.

Mr. Callahan wants me. Me. Can you believe it? Chubby Blaire. Ugly and awkward Blaire.

Unlovable Blaire.

I guess I'm not that ugly anymore. My body? What was considered fat as a child is now called boobs and ass. Guys want it. They want me. They want to touch me, grope me, feel me ... they want to screw me. And it feels good to be wanted ... so good. It makes me feel powerful, and like a potent drug spreading inside your bloodstream, I want more.

I need more.

"Hurry up," I say, not bothering to be shy or coy about it. I mean, he brought me here to have sex, right?

"Fuck, give me a second, Blaire. Trying to get the damn condom on my dick." As he rolls the rubber down his hard shaft, his eyes wander over my bare chest, my face, my spread legs. Shaking his head as if trying to clear his mind, he mutters, "You're so beautiful. I want you so much."

That's not the first time I've heard those words come out of a man's mouth. Josh tells me all the time how beautiful I am, how perfect I am, how much he wants me. But he's just a guy I randomly make out with. The words kind of lose their meaning when it's the same person saying them to you over and over again.

"Show me."

Those two words are all it takes for him to spread my legs wider with his hands and finally enter me. Pain shoots through my body, and a groan escapes my mouth when he covers my body with his. I feel his whole length inside me in one deep thrust.

"Christ, you're so tight."

He lifts both my legs, wrapping them around his lean waist and starts to thrust. Hard. It hurts. But I like the pain. It sobers me.

"Oh God … I love you, Blaire. I love you … I love you …" he pants in my ear.

And that's when reality comes crashing down on me. It hits me with the speed and blinding power of a torpedo, making me realize what I'm doing. What I'm giving away. And the man doesn't even know it.

What the hell am I doing?

Proving that you are your mother's daughter.

Making her proud.

The room is filled with the noises of the man grunting his pleasure and the wet slapping of our skin; it makes me want to gag. I want to throw up. Maybe it's the alcohol I drank.

Maybe it's self-disgust.

The initial pain is gone and now I just feel sore. And strange, like an out of body experience.

He lowers his face, his lips about to connect with mine, and I feel the bile rise inside my throat. I turn my face to the side, his kiss landing on my cheek. My eyes watch the way the lights in the bathroom illuminate all its used and dirty ugliness.

"Oh God, I'm going to come … I'm going to come … I'm going to come," he continues to pant in my ear, pumping in and out of my body. Before I know what's happening, he half screams and half groans, his body going tense on top of mine.

And just like that it's over. In less than five minutes I've managed to kill a part of me.

Our breathing evens and he pulls out, moving to stand up. I push myself up on my elbows to see him inspect his condom. It still glistens. By the time he lifts his eyes, connecting with mine, I've already wrapped my body with the duvet cover.

Confusion, shock, and pleasure reflect in those brown eyes. "I—I didn't know … I …" His hands go to his hair as we stare at each other. "I didn't know you were a virgin."

I shrug my shoulder carelessly, causing the duvet to slide down, exposing my bare breasts to him. His eyes immediately flare with lust. "It doesn't matter … I wanted it to be you."

And that's the truth.

"But—"

"But nothing. If it bothers you, then forget it happened. I already did," I say, ending the conversation.

This is my body. I will have the last word. Not him. Not anyone. This is my life. This is my decision.

Without giving myself a chance to doubt my next words, I turn to look at him in all his naked beauty, the gold wedding ring on his finger catching my attention. "Don't worry, Mr. Callahan … I won't tell your daughter that you fucked her classmate."

And with that, I seal my destiny.

59960894R00115

Made in the USA
Columbia, SC
11 June 2019